Captured!

A Boy Trapped in the Civil War

Captured!

A Boy Trapped in the Civil War

Mary Blair Immel

Indiana Historical Society Press
Indianapolis

Printed in Canada

This book is a publication of the
Indiana Historical Society Press
450 West Ohio Street
Indianapolis, Indiana 46202-3269 USA
www.indianahistory.org

Telephone orders 1-800-447-1830
Fax orders 317-234-0562
Orders by e-mail shop@indianahistory.org

The paper in this publication meets the minimum requirements of American National Standard for Information Sciences—Permanence of Paper for Printed Library Materials, ANSI Z39.48-1984. ∞

Library of Congress Cataloging-in-Publication Data

Immel, Mary Blair.
Captured : a boy trapped in the Civil War / Mary Blair Immel.
   p. cm.
Summary: Fourteen-year-old Johnny Ables, pressed into service in the
Confederate army, is forced to participate in a major Civil War battle and
ends up in an Indiana prison camp. Based on the true story of a real boy.
ISBN 0-87195-188-6 (alk. paper)
[1. Prisoners of war—Fiction. 2. United States—History—Civil War,
1861-1865—Fiction.] I. Title.
PZ7.I34Cap 2005
[Fic]—dc22

                   2005047491

This book is dedicated to
Samson Immel Stewart
and
Gretchen Virginia Stewart

Contents

Preface

Readers often ask where I get my ideas. My experience has been that ideas are everywhere, often in the most unexpected places. The inspiration for *Captured! A Boy Trapped in the Civil War* came when I was trying to find information for another book I was writing about a group of Confederate prisoners in Indiana.*

I discovered a petition written and signed by eighty-five soldiers from Mississippi. This petition outlined the basic facts concerning a young boy from Kentucky, who had been mistakenly captured and sent north to a prisoner of war camp. The petition asked that the boy be released. I could not help but wonder what happened to him. Was the boy freed from prison? Did he ever get home again?

I was busy with other projects at the time, but I could not put the story told by that petition out of my thoughts. I carried this idea around in my mind for years. Occasionally, I sought more information about this boy named Johnny Ables. His story was a good example of what can happen to a person who is in the wrong place at the wrong time.

Little by little, I began to learn what happened to Johnny, from the time he left home in Calloway County, Kentucky, in early February 1862. He experienced a lot of things. He was captured by Confederate soldiers who were retreating from a battle at Fort Henry in Tennessee. He was present during the Battle of Fort Donelson and endured a long, miserable journey from that Tennessee battlefield to Camp Morton, in Indianapolis. For nearly a month, he suffered a cold Northern winter in the prison camp, along with the Southern soldiers who had originally taken him prisoner.

The events of Johnny Ables's story are true. The people he met are real. I spent more than five years researching Johnny's story. I read many diaries, letters, journals, and books written by soldiers who were in the Battle of Fort Donelson and who were sent to Camp Morton Prison.

I traveled to Kentucky, Tennessee, and Mississippi, seeking information in large state archives and in small county libraries. I visited forts Henry and Donelson and walked those battlegrounds. I studied hundreds of military records. Readers who are interested can find a list of a few of the sources I read in a selected bibliography at the back of this book.

Although I now know most of Johnny's story, a few details are still missing. It is difficult for me to accept the fact that some loose ends may never be tied up neatly. The answers to all my questions may never be found. I suspect that long after this book is published, I will still be searching for clues, wanting to learn more. I hope that someday I will be able to fill in all the blanks.

When it came time for me to share Johnny's story, I wanted to remain as faithful to historical events as possible. However, I also wanted to make this story come alive for readers. Therefore, it was necessary for me to try to imagine what Johnny and the others who lived through that Civil War experience might have said, thought, and felt in those circumstances. That is why, in spite of all the research and documentation, I must call Johnny's story a historical novel rather than a work of non-fiction. It is, however, a true story.

* Beneath These Stones: The Story of the Confederate Prisoners in Lafayette, Indiana.

Strangers in the Woods

NEVER IN HIS WILDEST DREAMS could Johnny Ables have imagined what was in store for him that February morning in 1862 as he prepared to leave his small home in Calloway County, Kentucky. It didn't matter that Johnny was only fourteen years old and small for his age. He still considered himself to be the "man of the family" now that his father was dead. Johnny knew it was his responsibility to take care of his mother and his two little sisters. Whatever was necessary, Johnny would do.

The job that was required of him on this morning was to gather a wagonload of wood. The supply pile outside the doorway of their little house was getting low. His mother would soon need more in order to cook their meals and heat water to wash their clothing.

The pale sun had been up only a short time when Johnny went out to the barn and put down some feed for Ben and Jackie, the horses, to eat while he sharpened the ax. The last few days had been unusually warm for this time of the year. Nevertheless, he

took his father's old coat, which always hung on the hook by the
barn door, and put it on. He probably wouldn't need it today, but
he liked wearing it. Although it was too large for him and hung
loosely on his thin shoulders, it made Johnny feel as though his
father was still with him. He also put the old musket in the wagon
under the seat. His grandfather had carried that gun in the War of
1812. It was more than fifty years old, but Johnny took good care
of it, and he was a pretty good shot.

Johnny harnessed the horses and was climbing up onto the
seat of the wagon when his mother and two sisters came out of
the house. Ma carried a small tin bucket with a lid. She placed
it on the wagon seat beside him.

"There's some leftover pone in there and a bit of meat. Be
sure that you stop work at midday and take time to eat. You
need to keep up your strength."

Johnny grinned as he promised his mother that he would
do as she asked. He never missed a meal if he could help it.

Both of Johnny's little sisters wanted to go with him. He
knew they liked riding in the wagon, and he enjoyed having
them along. He sometimes took them with him when he had
to go into town or to the mill. Today, however, he was sorry
that he had to shake his head and tell them they couldn't go.

He knelt down and pulled the youngest girl up on his knee.
The nickname he had given this seven-year-old was "Tag,"
short for tag-along. This little yellow-haired sister had followed
close on his heels since the day she had learned to walk. He put
an arm around ten-year-old Sissy. He smiled at her and tousled
her strawberry colored hair.

This photograph shows how Johnny Ables's wagon and team of horses may have looked as Johnny set out to gather wood for his family.

"I wish you two could go with me, but I'm going to be working hard all day long. I won't have any time to stop and play games with you. You'd both get tired and want to come home."

He didn't mention that he would not have time to make sure they didn't wander off and get lost. Neither did he say that they might get hurt. He didn't want to have to keep a sharp eye out to make sure that they weren't in the way every time he swung his ax. Johnny couldn't always be certain a tree would fall exactly where he hoped it would. No, a woodcutting trip was no place for little girls.

"You two stay here and help Ma with the baking."

Sissy still didn't seem happy at being left behind, but she sighed and said, "We'll make something special for you to eat when you get home."

"Yes, something real special," Tag echoed.

"I'm counting on it," Johnny told them.

Johnny flicked the reins and made a little "chuck-chuck" sound with his tongue. Ben and Jackie moved forward, and he was on his way. Johnny thought the rickety old wagon sounded as if it would fall apart as it bumped over the rutted lane. It had put in a lot of years of hard use. He turned to look back at his mother and sisters. They were waving at him, and he waved back.

The sun felt good and warmed his back as he bounced along on the seat of the wagon. A few crows were making a racket as they fought over some choice morsel they had discovered. A flash of red crossed his path as a brilliantly colored cardinal swooped past. A rabbit darted out of the underbrush, then ducked back quickly as Johnny passed by on the wagon seat. Squirrels scrambled around the trunks of large trees, pausing for a few seconds to cock their heads and stare at him with their bright brown eyes.

Johnny hummed a little tune as he headed in a southerly direction. He had heard some of the men at church talking about a place where a big storm had blown some trees down. It would be easier to get all the wood he needed if he didn't have to fell any trees. If he could pick up a good-sized load, there might be enough wood for his family and maybe even some to sell to neighbors. That would bring in a welcome bit of money.

Johnny knew that his mother would be glad to have a few coins to buy things she needed at the store. Maybe Ma might even be able to get some calico to make dresses for herself and his sisters. Perhaps there would be enough left over for her to make a shirt for him. The one he wore today had patches sewn on top of patches.

Life had not been easy for the Ables family since Pa had died. Sometimes Ma had a few chicken eggs to trade for a bit of lard and other necessary items at the store. If she was lucky, she was hired to do some fancy sewing for one of the ladies in town who admired her fine handiwork with a needle. Although Ma put in long hours making tiny stitches in delicate fabrics, she wasn't paid much money in return for her efforts. Usually, the Ables family had to make do with the vegetables they could raise in their garden, instead of store-bought food. Once in a while, Ma would prepare an old hen to have for dinner. When he had time, Johnny would take the musket and go hunting for a rabbit or a squirrel to add to the stew pot. He'd much rather be hunting than picking worms off the tobacco plants. Because of his small size working with tobacco was about the only thing the farmers would hire him to do.

Johnny's thoughts were interrupted as he came to the river. He would have to cross it in order to get to the place where he'd heard there was good wood down on the ground. He headed toward the ford, where it was usually passable. He was not concerned that he would be crossing over a state border. That sort of thing didn't seem important to Johnny. What did it matter whether the downed trees were in the state of Kentucky or Tennessee?

Johnny had sometimes lived in neighboring Henry County, Tennessee. When Ma had her hands full of taking care of Pa before he coughed himself to death, the Ables's children had been sent to live with family and friends. Johnny had often stayed with Aunt Mellie and Uncle James on their place down at Ratterree's Landing. Aunt Mellie was a good sort and treated him like she was his own mother. Ma said it was because Aunt Mellie had only one son of her own and yearned for more children.

So, Johnny felt equally at home in Tennessee and in Kentucky. All that mattered to him today was that he find wood. But, Johnny found more than wood. He found unexpected trouble, or, rather, trouble found him.

After crossing the river, Johnny followed a small stream and reached the spot he had heard about. There was no doubt that this was the place. He smiled. He liked what he saw. The leaves were shriveled and brown now, but he easily recognized the shaggy bark of the hickory and the pale gray trunks of white oak trees. The men at church had been right; there were a good many trees down. He could only imagine what kind of a storm had blown through here to uproot some of these large trees. Of course, there was no way he could handle them by himself, but when they had come crashing down, many limbs had been broken off. This meant that he would have to do very little chopping to make them a size he could manage. He examined several limbs to see if they were still green and felt the wood to see if it had dried out. Johnny was confident that it would burn well without much aging.

He knew he was going to get a good load of wood today, but it wouldn't be easy. Johnny started to work immediately, dragging several large limbs over to the wagon and wrestling them up onto its bed. He would wait until he returned home to cut them into more usable lengths.

Johnny worked for a couple of hours, hauling and lifting, until the wagon was full up to the first railing. He worked up a fine sweat. There was something satisfying about that. Johnny liked doing good, hard work, even though he knew his arms and back would be sore the next day. Maybe such work would help him get the kind of muscles his cousin Asa had.

He took off Pa's coat and tossed it up onto the wagon seat. Then he walked a few steps to a stream that sparkled in the sunlight, knelt down on a flat rock, leaned over, and cupped his hands to scoop up a drink of water. It tasted good. Johnny was getting another drink when he heard a strange sound.

It was a low buzzing. Could there be a bee tree nearby? He stood up and looked around eagerly. Ma and the girls would be pleased if he brought some honey with him when he came home. That would be a special treat for them all. The buzzing seemed to be getting closer but Johnny didn't see any sign of bees. He did see movement in the trees a short distance away, however. Johnny realized then that the sound was not bees at all but men's voices. He wiped his mouth on the back of his hand and stared. There were men in the woods, a lot of them, and they were coming in his direction.

"Well, now. Just looky here what we got," said a deep voice. Johnny whirled, surprised to see a rough-looking man standing behind him, grinning. "I think Providence has smiled on us."

Another man stepped out from behind a tree. "This young'un don't amount to much, but these horses and that wagon load of wood will come in right handy."

Johnny looked frantically to his right and then to his left. Who were these men who had managed to sneak up on him this way? What were they going to do to him? He thought about making a break and running from them. But, before he could move, more men emerged from the woods.

One of the men grabbed the horses' reins and said to Johnny, "Come on young feller. I reckon the captain will be right glad to see what we found."

Where were they taking him? What did they want with him? Johnny tried to speak, but his heart was thudding. He couldn't manage to say a word. All he could do was follow along behind his horses and wagon while these strange men led the way.

2

Captured!

AS HE TRUDGED ALONG, Johnny had a good chance to size up the men who had taken charge of him and his horses and wagon. They wore walnut brown pants and jackets. Some of them had blanket rolls strapped to their backs. A few had cooking pots swinging from their packs. But the thing that bothered Johnny most was that they all carried muskets.

It wasn't until he was in the midst of a large group of the men that he realized they were soldiers. Confederate soldiers.

"We got us a prize here, Captain," the first man called out.

The captain turned out to be a man outfitted in a fine gray uniform. The jacket had two rows of gold buttons that glistened in the sun, and its sleeves were adorned with scrolls of gold braid.

The captain looked at Johnny and walked around the wagon. He ran his hands over the horses' flanks and nodded approvingly. "I'd say you boys did yourself proud," he said. Then he looked up at the position of the sun in the sky and said, "We'll go another hour before we stop. Bring your catch along. Now, move out."

One of the soldiers motioned for Johnny to get back up on the wagon seat. The soldiers fell into line marching, taking Johnny with them. Johnny should have told the soldiers that they didn't have a right to make him go with them. He should have explained to them how much his mother needed him at home. She would have no way of knowing what had happened to him. He should have insisted that he needed to take his wagon and horses with the load of wood back to Calloway County. But, Johnny didn't say any of this. He was just too thunderstruck at what was happening to him, and he thought that these men would not react kindly to a challenge.

When the captain finally called a halt, the men gathered in a small clearing. Johnny stayed on the wagon seat and didn't climb down to join them.

At first Johnny thought they were going to have their midday meal. He took the cover off his tin bucket holding the food that his mother had sent with him that morning. Then he noticed that the soldiers didn't seem to have much to eat. He didn't have enough food to share with everyone, so he broke off only a small bit of his corn bread. He didn't eat any of the bacon Ma had put in his bucket. He would save that for later. Johnny put the lunch bucket under the wagon bed near his musket and covered both with Pa's coat.

As Johnny sat watching the men, one of them nodded his head in the direction of the wagon and said in a loud voice: "I'm hungry enough to eat a horse." Surely they were just funning him, but Johnny couldn't be sure just what such hungry men would do.

"Maybe tonight we can get us a rabbit or a possum to cook over that load of wood," another soldier said.

Some of the men sat on logs. One was whittling on a stick. Two or three of them had taken off their shoes and were soaking their feet in the stream. Most of them stretched out in the shade and closed their eyes. The ones that were not sleeping talked among themselves. From their conversations, Johnny learned something of why these soldiers happened to be in this place.

They had come across country from Fort Henry, not far from the borderline between Kentucky and Tennessee. For the past several days the Confederate soldiers were part of a garrison that tried to stand off Union gunboats on the Tennessee River. When it became apparent to their leaders that they could not hold the fort, their commander ordered them to leave so they could escape capture. They would be needed elsewhere. This is why they were trudging wearily eastward along the path leading toward Fort Donelson on the Cumberland River. Ordinarily, it was a ten-mile march between the two points, but these men had come by a roundabout route that was twice the distance of the direct one.

Johnny realized that the men were not only tired and hungry, but their spirits were low because of what had happened back at Fort Henry. The soldiers grumbled about how it wasn't right that they didn't get to stay and fight the Yankees. They contented themselves with the thought that if they could get

Bombardment of Fort Henry, Tennessee, February 6, 1862.

to Fort Donelson in time, they would have another chance to show their bravery and determination. They could swell the ranks of the Confederate forces that would soon be defending against Union soldiers who were also headed in the direction of Donelson.

While Johnny sat there he had a wild idea. Maybe he could get away while the men were resting and thinking about other things. He could just slap the reins and let Ben and Jackie run the wagon out of there as fast as they could go. But, would his horses be fast enough to make such a dash? Johnny doubted that this would be the case, not when they were dragging a heavy load of wood. The awful thought entered his mind that this old rattle-trap of a wagon would probably shake itself apart if he did try to make a run for it. Besides, the soldiers might grab their guns to try to stop him. They might really shoot the horses. If that happened, what would he do? Johnny sighed and discarded this idea of trying to escape. He'd have to think of something else.

Maybe he could slide quietly off the back of the wagon and slip away through the underbrush. How far could he get before they noticed he was gone? Then he realized that even if he did manage to escape, he'd be leaving Ben and Jackie and the wagon behind. How could he and his ma manage without them?

Finally, Johnny decided that if he were patient, he would be all right once they arrived at Fort Donelson. He would unload the wood and gladly give it to the soldiers. After that, what need would they have for him? He wasn't a soldier. He had no training. They would just let him go home, wouldn't they? He held onto that thought as the men were ordered to march on once more.

As he rumbled along, Johnny couldn't help but remember how the folks back home in Calloway County were so divided among themselves because of the war. He knew of some brothers who were fighting in armies on opposite sides. There had been parades in town for the boys who had joined the Southern army. There had been band music and a lot of "speechifying" by important people in town. Many of the ladies had made brightly colored flags for the companies of soldiers to carry into battle. Many of the young girls in the county had followed the lines of soldiers as they marched away, promising to write to the boys everyday. Some girls even tucked their handkerchiefs or photographs into the soldiers' pockets.

There had been a few fellows who went off to fight for the Union army, but most folks that Johnny knew were sympathetic to the South. Those who weren't kept their mouths shut for the most part.

Johnny had wondered what it would be like to be a soldier. The sound of the drums made his heart beat a bit faster. He knew that lots of boys his age dreamed about how exciting it

Effect of gunboat shells on Confederate soldiers in the woods.

would be to wear a uniform, carry a musket, and go off to war. Johnny's older cousin, Asa, had joined up. Aunt Mellie put on a brave show as her only son marched off with the 10th Tennessee. But, later, Johnny had seen her in the summer kitchen, dabbing her tears with her apron.

No, Johnny couldn't even think about joining the army. Ma and the girls needed him. Who would take care of them if he were to sign up as a soldier? Now, unexpectedly, whether he wanted to or not, Johnny Ables was moving with the Confederate army that was heading toward a face-off with the Union army.

The hours passed and every turn of the wagon wheels measured off the distance Johnny was being forced to go farther and farther from Calloway County. His thoughts turned to his mother and sisters. He knew they would be waiting anxiously for him to come home. Most certainly his mother would be worried as the afternoon sun sank lower in the western sky and he had not returned. How many times would Sissy and Tag walk down the lane to look in both directions, hoping to catch a glimpse of him? When it got dark, Ma would light a candle and put it in the window to help him find his way home. Try as he might, Johnny could think of no way to escape his captors, and he could think of no way to let his family know where he was.

The wood that Johnny had loaded into his wagon earlier that morning made several fine campfires when the soldiers stopped for the night. It didn't take long for the famished soldiers to cook and eat what little bit of food they had. One of the men called to Johnny, "Come on down off that wagon seat, Sprout."

The man handed him a greasy bit of bacon to eat. Johnny nodded gratefully and then felt guilty when he thought about his tin lunch bucket hidden beneath the wagon seat. He knew he ought to share his food, but he eased his conscience with the thought that he would need it the next day if he were allowed to go home.

After their meager meal, the soldiers warmed themselves near the fire, talking among themselves. Johnny sat on a log and listened. These men didn't seem to be bad sorts. In fact, it was downright friendly that they had asked him to sit with them and warm himself at their campfire. He liked the way the soldiers had started calling him "Sprout." It made him feel like he was one of them. For a while he forgot that they had taken him with them against his will.

As Johnny looked around the circle at the campfire, he noticed that the soldiers were of all ages. Some of the older men like William Cade talked about their families. Cade had left a wife and three children back home in Mississippi. Johnny could tell that all of the men missed their loved ones as much as he was missing his.

Several of the soldiers were young boys. One was just a year older than Johnny. Surprisingly, that boy had the very same first name. He was Johnny Roche. Johnny Ables wondered how Johnny Roche had been allowed to enlist in the army when he was underage.

"I didn't have to tell an out-and-out lie," young Roche insisted. "But, I did use a little trick that some other fellers told me about."

Johnny waited. Roche seemed to enjoy telling this story.

"I wrote the numbers '1' and '8' on a piece of paper and put it inside my shoe. When the recruiting officer asked me if I was old enough to join, I said, 'Well, I'm over eighteen.'"

The men all laughed, but Johnny didn't understand. His face must have shown that he was puzzled, because Roche explained. "Don't you get it? The paper with the numbers '1' and '8' was in my shoe. I was standing on top of it. So, I could honestly say I was over eighteen, and not have to tell a downright lie about my age."

The soldiers laughed again and one of them said, "Sprout, you'll do well to watch out what you hear from young Private Roche."

"Well, there's one thing you had better believe when I say it," Roche bragged. "Ours is the best company in the 4th Mississippi Regiment, and we've got the best name, too."

"That's for certain," a soldier named Hector Hamilton agreed. "We're the Red Invincibles."

"Yes, siree," added Dudley Wallace. "We're the Invincibles because nobody can beat us. And, we're called the Red Invincibles because our captain is W. C. Red."

"That's kind of a little joke," Roche explained to Johnny, "using our captain's name that way."

"Except it ain't no joke about us being invincible," Solon Alexander added. "At least, we'd be invincible if anybody would let us stay and fight."

That comment set off more grumbling among the soldiers about how they had been ordered to leave Fort Henry without giving them a chance to get into battle.

"That's all right, boys," Wallace said. "We're going to get a chance to show them what we can do once we get to Fort Donelson."

Johnny sat and stared at the fire as it dwindled down to glowing embers. The conversation was like the fire; it just sort of wore itself out. Most of the soldiers rolled up in their blankets and went to sleep.

Johnny didn't have a blanket, so he climbed up in the back of the wagon and put Pa's coat over him. One of the soldiers was playing a song on his mouth organ. Johnny thought he'd heard it before, but he couldn't think of the name of it. It was a sad sounding melody, and it made Johnny lonesome for home and Ma, Tag, and Sissy. As he drifted off to sleep, he hoped that the next day the soldiers would let him take Ben and Jackie with the wagon and head back home to Kentucky.

3

No Escape

AT DAYLIGHT, any idea Johnny may have had that the soldiers of the 4th Mississippi would allow him to go home faded. He was awakened by the sound of men preparing for another day's march. It took a little time before Johnny realized where he was and remembered what had happened to him the day before.

He heard Captain Red's voice. "Let's go, boys. We need to be on our way. There will be plenty for us to do when we get to Fort Donelson. We've got to get dug in before the Yankees arrive."

Loud pounding on the side of his wagon followed this announcement. "That means you, too, Sprout."

Johnny rubbed the sleep from his eyes and saw Wallace looking at him over the wagon rails. "You'd best be getting those horses in harness. You need to be ready to roll right soon. If we get to Fort Donelson before sundown, you'll have time to get another load of wood."

Johnny thought about saying, "I'm not going with you. I'm going back home." He didn't say it, though. The words stuck in his throat. These soldiers were not the kind of men you wanted to argue with. They were tired, hungry, and disgruntled. Besides, Johnny knew they needed the horses and wagon more than they needed him. Even if they did allow him to go, he knew he'd go alone and on foot. He wasn't ready to walk away leaving Ben and Jackie or the wagon. He would bide his time, watching and waiting until he saw a good opportunity to escape from his captors.

Johnny clambered down from the wagon and went to get the horses from the place he had tethered them for the night. "I'm sorry, fellers," Johnny said to Ben and Jackie as he slipped the bridles over their noses and ears. "I don't have any oats to give you. You'll have to manage with what you can find to graze on along the way."

The horses snorted, their breath steaming in the early morning dampness. He rubbed their ears and patted their flanks. He hoped they understood. Ben and Jackie weren't the only ones who didn't get their breakfast. Johnny didn't have anything to eat this morning either. No one did.

The soldiers formed a loose column four abreast and began to move forward. Johnny, on the wagon, brought up the rear, but there was no way he could manage an escape. Just before the march began, Captain Red said, "Williams, get up there and ride on the wagon with Sprout."

The soldier said, "Yes, sir," and dutifully climbed up onto the wooden seat beside Johnny.

At first Johnny thought the soldier was there to guard him and make sure he didn't try to escape. Johnny kept glancing sideways to see if the soldier was watching him. Williams, however, wasn't paying any attention to Johnny. He seemed to be having his own troubles. His arms were clasped tightly over his stomach. He doubled over and groaned each time the wagon wheels jounced over rough ground. Then, with some effort, Williams would sit up again as straight as he could, only to repeat the motion with the next jarring bump of the wagon. The day was warming up, but it was not hot. Yet, there were beads of sweat on the soldier's red face. Johnny could see that Williams was not feeling well.

"I'm sorry it's such a bumpy ride," Johnny said, trying to avoid as many ruts as he could.

Williams said, "Don't worry about me. There's nothing you can do. Besides, this is easier for me than it would be if I had to walk."

As Johnny's wagon rolled over the hilly landscape through woods and ravines, he noticed that he could not see much of what lay ahead or behind him. That seemed to be the way he felt about his life right now. There was a terrible uncertainty about what was going to happen next. He had no way to know what lay ahead or to figure out how to make things right again.

On this day, the soldiers did not stop at midday. They hardly paused at all to rest. They arrived at the little town of Dover, Tennessee, while it was still early afternoon. Fort Donelson was only a short distance away. It was an earthwork fortification, but it was not yet complete. There were two river batteries with

The water batteries at Fort Donelson overlooked the Cumberland River. The guns were protected by thick breastworks, the tops of which were covered with coffee sacks filled with sand.

twelve heavy guns on high ground overlooking the Cumberland River. About four hundred small log huts sheltered the three thousand Confederate soldiers who were stationed there. In addition, the woods were now alive with other regiments that had come to reinforce the fort.

Johnny watched as soldiers from other companies of the 4th Mississippi who had arrived earlier greeted the Red Invincibles with cheers. The men of Company C were directed where they should put up their tents.

There was a young soldier who seemed to know everything or thought he did. He was intent on telling everything he knew to each new group of arrivals. His words flowed like a great tidal wave, threatening to drown everyone.

"Over there's the 41st Mississippi. Look through the trees, and you can see the 30th Tennessee. There's boys here from Kentucky, Arkansas, and some from Virginia. Everybody's digging in. We got here before the Yankees. There's no way they can stop us this time." The great talker paused for just a moment to take a breath and looked directly at Johnny. "Well, now, you got a wagon. That's going to come in handy. You'll be hauling wood for everybody."

Johnny saw groups of soldiers wearing regular Confederate army uniforms of gray wool and some of butternut brown. There were a great many, however, who wore homespun shirts and homemade pants of jeans cloth. All around him, these soldiers were busy setting up their campsites.

Johnny watched with interest as one soldier pulled a section of heavy white canvas from his knapsack. His comrade did the same. They buttoned these two pieces together at the top. This large piece was then slung over a rope the men had tied between two tree trunks that were fairly close together. The soldiers pegged the canvas down on the sides, stretching it tightly to form a two-man dog tent. Soldiers who couldn't find two good trees together hunted for a sturdy tree limb to plant in the ground and use as a center pole.

"That's the whole shebang," one of the soldiers said to his friend, with satisfaction, as he surveyed their handiwork. Johnny looked around as row upon row of these tents appeared in the woods like mushrooms in springtime. The different regiments identified their areas with banners hanging from flagpoles stuck in the ground. It was a colorful sight that reminded Johnny of the county fair back home.

Once the tents were up, the men of Company C began unpacking their knapsacks. Johnny was amazed at the amount

A reproduction of one of the log huts used by the Confederate army while stationed at Fort Donelson in Tennessee.

of equipment the soldiers could jam into those sacks or tie on the bedrolls they carried over their backs. Some had cooking pots or skillets that they had brought from home. One clever soldier had bent a ramrod at one end to form a hook so that he could hang his pot over the fire. Everyone, except Johnny, had a tin cup. These were issued to each fighting man by the Confederate government, along with a knife, fork, and spoon. Each soldier had also been given a Bible.

What weren't supplied to the soldiers were playing cards. Many soldiers had created their own, using any stray piece of cardboard or heavy paper they could get their hands on. Many of the men had smoking pipes and tobacco pouches. Some had small diaries to make note of what had happened to them each day. There were musical instruments, mouth organs, mouth harps, and a few fiddles.

Johnny noticed that the officers' tents, like their uniforms, were much better than those of the ordinary soldiers. The officers wore well-tailored uniforms, often with gold braid trim and shiny buttons. Some of the officers' tents were large enough for a bed and even a writing table. More than one officer had a black servant to put things in order.

"All right, boys," shouted Captain Red. "We're going to put our rifle pits here, here, and here." As he talked, the captain walked to each of the places, broke off a small tree branch, and stuck it in the ground to show his soldiers where they should dig. "Dig those trenches as deep as you can, and press tree limbs along the insides to keep the dirt from caving in on you. Then, pile the branches up in front like you were making a duck blind. The better job you do now, the safer you'll be when those minié balls start flying."

There were not enough shovels for everyone, so the soldiers had to take turns. Johnny heard a lot of complaining about the lack of equipment.

Williams climbed down gingerly off Johnny's wagon and untied a patchwork quilt that he carried on his back. He unrolled it, spread it under a tree, and lay down.

The talker asked, "What's the matter with him? Has he got the measles?" He didn't wait for an answer before he volunteered the information that a lot of the soldiers who had been

These fortifications inside Confederate lines are similar to the rifle pits that the Red Invincibles dug to protect themselves during the Battle at Fort Donelson.

stationed at Fort Donelson had suffered from measles during the winter.

The captain called out to Johnny, "Sprout, start gathering wood. We're going to need lots of it tonight."

An idea flickered across Johnny's mind. This might be his chance. There was so much activity and confusion that no one would notice if he rode away deep into the trees. If anyone tried to stop him, he could say that he had been sent to get wood. All he had to do was to keep going farther and farther until he was out of sight. Then he could head northward, following the river, until he crossed into Kentucky and was on his way home with nobody the wiser.

Johnny hurried to get back up onto the wagon seat. He slapped the reins, and Ben and Jackie moved obediently forward. Johnny's heart was pounding with excitement. His mouth was dry. Don't go too fast, he told himself. Don't look back. That will seem suspicious. Just act as though you really are going off to get wood. Behind him someone shouted, but Johnny did not turn around. He pretended he hadn't heard, that he didn't think anyone was calling to him.

Suddenly he was aware of someone running alongside the wagon, waving his hat. It was Johnny Roche.

"Hold up there," Roche called to him. "The captain told me to come along with you."

Johnny noticed that Roche wasn't carrying his musket. He couldn't shoot Johnny if he made a break for it. But, Johnny knew that there were too many other soldiers around to try to make the escape he had planned. Johnny squeezed his eyes together tightly to keep back tears of disappointment. Would he ever have another opportunity like this to get back home? He sighed and hauled up on the reins. The horses stopped and waited while Roche climbed up onto the seat beside Johnny.

"Captain said there's a good stand of open timber over in that direction," Roche pointed. Johnny took a deep breath and turned the horses in the direction Roche had indicated.

4

New Friends

JOHNNY ABLES AND JOHNNY ROCHE worked side by side the rest of the afternoon. Roche was a sturdy young man and seemed tireless. The load of wood in the wagon grew and grew.

Finally, Johnny had to say, "I think this is all my horses can pull. They're tuckered out. They're not so young any more and haven't had much to eat."

The two boys sat on the back of the wagon and rested before heading back to where the 4th Mississippi was camped.

Roche mopped his face with a red handkerchief. "We're going to make a good fight out of this," he said. "We're going to make those Yankees wish they'd never tangled with us. This isn't going to be like Fort Henry. We've got the advantage this time."

As he listened to Roche's words, Johnny realized that he might find himself right smack in the middle of a battle. Somehow that thought had not crossed his mind until now. He tried to imagine what it would be like, but he couldn't. All he knew was that it was a frightening thought. He wasn't a soldier. This wouldn't be like shooting rabbits. What would be expected of him? What would happen to him? He wished he could ask Roche, but he didn't want to be thought a coward.

"You hungry?" Johnny asked, and then thought what a silly question that was. Of course Roche was hungry. They were all hungry. "I've got a little bit of corn bread and meat I've been saving in my lunch bucket."

Johnny got the tin bucket from under the wagon seat. He pried the lid off the top and smelled the meat. It had been there a couple of days, but it seemed all right. He handed Roche half the meat and half the corn pone. Roche nodded his thanks. The two boys ate slowly, making the little bit of food last as long as possible. The pone was dry, but he was so hungry, Johnny didn't mind.

While they were eating, Johnny saw something moving behind one of the trees some distance away. Roche saw it, too, and whispered, "Look, what's that over there?"

It didn't seem large enough to be a man. Johnny squinted. "Some sort of critter. Maybe a deer."

"Too small for a deer. Might be a fox," Roche answered.

A moment later the critter emerged into full sight, and both boys laughed.

"It's a dog," Johnny said. "Just a mutt, I reckon."

"I had me a dog back home," Roche said. "I couldn't go anywhere that he didn't follow me. He was a good coon dog. I sure miss him."

Roche got down on one knee, whistled, and called out, "Here boy. Come and see me."

The dog stopped still and stared at Roche, but he didn't respond to Roche's call. Roche held out a bit of the precious food he had in his hand. "You hungry, boy? Come on."

Still the dog refused to move. Instead he sat down and looked at Roche. The dog almost seemed to be daring Roche to try to catch him.

Johnny could sense that Roche was frustrated that the dog would not come to him. He tried hard to keep from laughing as Roche did his best to get the dog to respond. The dog tilted his head first to one side and then to the other, his bright eyes watching Roche. The dog's little red tongue hung from one corner of his half-open mouth. By now Roche was down on both hands and knees pretending to lunge at the dog. To Johnny it looked as though the dog was grinning at Roche's antics.

Then they heard a distinctive sound from the woods, three short, sharp whistles. The dog jumped up immediately and scampered back in the direction from which he had just come. A man's voice called out: "Where have you been, old fellow?" A soldier emerged from a thicket with the dog at his heels. When the soldier stopped, the dog stopped and sat obediently at his side.

"Is that your dog?" Roche asked.

"Sure is," the soldier said.

"You sure got him trained right smart," Roche said admiringly. "He wouldn't come to me no matter what I did. I offered him food but he wouldn't budge an inch."

"He's a regular little trooper," the soldier said. "He only takes orders from me."

The dog waited obediently by his master's side, looking up at him.

"What's that pouch hanging around his neck?" Johnny wanted to know.

"That's his haversack. Every good soldier's got one, so I had one made up for him. He carries his grub in it, just like I carry my vittles in mine."

"Well, I never saw the like of it," Roche said.

It was easy to see that Roche was itching to get his hands on that dog. The soldier must have sensed it, too, and said, "Okay, Frank. Go give him a 'hello.'"

The dog looked up at his master. When the soldier nodded, the dog bounded toward Roche, nearly knocking him over. Roche cradled the dog in his arms and scratched his ears. The dog gave Roche's face a good tongue-washing.

"Did I hear you call that dog Frank?" Johnny asked.

The soldier nodded. "Yep, that's his name all right. Good ole Frank."

Roche played with the dog for a couple of minutes, and then the soldier said, "I reckon we'd best be getting back to our camp now."

"What regiment are you with?" Johnny asked.

"We're the 2nd Kentucky, right over yonder," the soldier said. "Company B." He gave three more short, sharp whistles, and Frank broke free from Roche and obediently ran to his master's side. Then the two of them went back through the woods the way they had come.

Roche and Johnny stood watching the dog and his master

depart. Roche said, "Now who ever heard of a dog called Frank?"

Johnny looked away quickly as he saw Roche pass his sleeve across his eyes and take a deep breath.

Roche suddenly changed the subject. "Where do you come from?" he asked Johnny.

"I was born in Calloway County, Kentucky," Johnny said. "But I've lived in northern Tennessee, too. That's not far from where I was cutting wood yesterday."

"Is your pa in the army?" Roche asked.

Johnny paused before he answered. It was still hard for him to talk about his father, especially to strangers. "My pa died a while back."

Roche didn't speak for a moment, and then he said, "My pa is dead, too."

Johnny couldn't think of anything to say, but he felt that the fact that both of their fathers were dead somehow brought them closer. He hoped that Roche could understand how he felt. Maybe Roche would know how much Johnny missed his home and family. Maybe he wouldn't say anything if Johnny tried to leave right now. But, Johnny decided it was probably just wishful thinking to expect that he could escape. Besides, Roche might get into trouble for letting Johnny get away.

The two boys stood quietly for a while, neither looking at the other, each wrapped up in his own distant thoughts. Finally, Roche stood up. "We'd best be getting on back to camp now. It'll be time to start the fires, and they'll need this wood." Johnny nodded and climbed wearily up on the wagon seat.

As he helped unload the wood at the different camp sites, Johnny thought how strange things were. He couldn't help liking these soldiers who had taken charge of him. They weren't mean to him. Of course, they had taken him along against his will, but they hadn't tied him up to keep him from escaping. Still, in a way, he was their prisoner all the same because he couldn't get away from them. They made him go out and collect wood for them. He worked so hard his entire body ached. On the other hand, they let him sit with them at night by the campfire and shared whatever little bit of food they had.

That night after he tethered Ben and Jackie nearby, he sat with the soldiers by the fire. He sensed that a change had come over the men. The first night they had been downhearted about

A Confederate campsite.

what had happened at Fort Henry. Then they had talked in soft voices about their families and played melancholy songs.

Now, Johnny could see dozens of campfires flickering through the woods. It was almost festive. He could hear a different tone to the conversations. There was a confidence, even a certainty that things were going their way. Johnny thought it had something to do with what Roche had said earlier this afternoon about having the advantage. The men were getting ready to fight, and they were sure they were going to win. Tonight, their voices were heartier. They were in good spirits. They told stories that made them roar with laughter.

"I recollect one old boy who joined up when we did. He had to be the laziest man in Mississippi. Whenever there was marchin' and drillin' to be done, he'd hide out somewhere and take a nap. Well, one time we peeled a pokeweed—you know how slickery that is. Then, we tied a string around one end of it and tied the other end of it to his ankle while he was snoring away. We stuck that pokeweed up his pant leg and then shouted, 'Snake!' He woke up with a start—must have jumped three feet in the air when he felt that pokeweed. He started to run, and that weed on a string followed along behind him, so he couldn't get rid of it. He ran till he finally just fell down kickin' and screaming. He kept shoutin', 'Where's my gun? Where's my gun? Somebody shoot that thing!' He decided then that he wasn't cut out to be a soldier. Captain agreed, and he was let to go home."

The men were still telling stories and laughing when Johnny went to bed. He would like to have stayed to listen, but he was too tired. For a second night, Johnny slept in his wagon wrapped up in his pa's coat. He lay on his back and looked up at the stars. He wished that somehow he could let his ma know that he was all right—well, as all right as anybody in his circumstances could be. He wasn't sick or hurt or anything like that. Yet, in another way, he was glad she didn't know where he was. After all, if she knew he was at Fort Donelson waiting for the Yankees to arrive, he wasn't sure how comforting that would be.

As Johnny lay there in the light of the campfire, he scratched two marks on one of the sideboards of his wagon, one mark for each night he had been away from home. For the next few days, Johnny's life at the campsite was much the same. He could hardly believe it when he scratched a fifth mark on the wagon's sideboard.

5

The Earth Shakes

ON THE SIXTH MORNING that Johnny Ables was with the soldiers of the 4th Mississippi at Fort Donelson, Tennessee, he felt the earth move. A jolting thump nearly knocked him off his feet. The ground-shaking thud was accompanied by what sounded like a clap of thunder. His heart pounded when this happened again and again and again. It was like nothing he had ever felt or heard before in his entire life. Johnny looked around to see what the soldiers were making of it.

"It's cannons!" one of them shouted.

"The Yankee gunboats must have come up the Cumberland River," said another. "They're firing on the fort."

Johnny saw William Cade running for one of the newly dug rifle pits. "Hurry up, Sprout," Cade shouted. "Run for it if you don't want to get your tail feathers singed."

Johnny followed Cade and several others who were diving into the pits for safety. He hunched down in the trench, staying as low as he could. The earth shook even harder when the

Confederate cannons from Fort Donelson began to answer the Yankee guns.

Johnny was glad to see Roche crawling along the trench and hunching down beside him. "We got plenty of this when we were at Fort Henry," Roche said. "The Yankees won that one, but we're in better position here."

Johnny nodded. His mouth was so dry, he didn't seem to be able to speak aloud. He stayed in the trenches with the soldiers from Mississippi the entire day as the pounding by the gunboats and the answering cannons from the fort continued to shake the earth. Off and on, the men heard popping sounds from nearby skirmishes between the Confederate and Union soldiers.

This gunboat, used at the battle of Fort Donelson, was the first ironclad gunboat built in America. It was "armed, supplied, officered and manned" jointly by the Union army and navy.

In the late afternoon, the weather suddenly turned colder, much colder. Johnny had left his pa's coat in the wagon, so he had nothing to wrap around himself—not that it would have done him much good. A downpour of sleety rain drenched him and the miserable soldiers to the skin. As the day darkened and turned to night, there was relief from the cannons and guns, but the weather proved to be an unrelenting enemy. The soldiers dared not try to light a fire as the smallest flickering light made them a target for Union snipers. There was no way to get dry or warm. Johnny huddled with the others, wet and shivering in the frigid darkness.

The temperature that night dropped to ten degrees. The mud became ice. Roche removed the old homespun blanket that he carried in a roll over his shoulder and wrapped it around Johnny and himself as they huddled together for warmth. Soon, they were both covered by a white blanket of snow.

The next day was brutally cold. Nervous and expectant, Johnny and the soldiers huddled in misery in the trenches. Around mid-afternoon, the awful sound of canon fire erupted again, filling Johnny's heart with dread. Just when he thought it would never end, the thundering noise stopped abruptly.

In the sudden silence, Johnny heard a new sound in the distance. He and Roche looked at each other, trying to understand what was happening. As the sound came nearer, Johnny discovered that it was cheering. The joyful shouting grew louder as one company after another joined in the celebration. Word passed along from one line of trenches to another. He saw soldiers climbing out of the trenches and throwing their hats in the air and yelling at the top of their lungs. "We did it!

We did it!" The Confederate cannons from Fort Donelson had disabled the Yankee gunboats on the river. That was not the end of the fight, however.

After another bitterly cold night, Johnny awoke to the sound of a menacing rattle that was worse than some monstrous snake scrabbling about in dried leaves. That rat-a-tat-tat was the deadly sound of hundreds of muskets shooting rapidly, one after the other. The noise surrounded him as soldiers fired and took fire from Union soldiers across the ravine to the south of their lines. Then the Confederate soldiers heard cannons, not from the river, but from the Union lines opposite them on the battlefield. The cannon balls slammed into the earth nearby throwing clods of dirt and sometimes even rocks into the rifle pits.

Johnny covered his head with both arms as a cannon ball flew past. It made a whooshing sound as though some giant were blowing air out of his cheeks, and it seemed to suck the breath out of Johnny's lungs. He wanted to look, but he felt a lot safer with his eyes covered. He finally did look up when he heard a sharp splintering sound. A large tree limb had been hit by a cannon ball, and it came crashing to the ground not far from the rifle pit.

Johnny gasped for breath as he felt the suffocating smoke of battle roll over him. It stung his eyes and burned his nose and throat when he tried to breathe. He gagged on the smell of it. There was nothing he could do to get away from it. Would it never stop? Roche, Cade, Wallace, and the others fired their guns at an enemy they could not see sometimes, but at least they were doing something. Johnny felt completely helpless. He had left his musket in the wagon, and he had seen the wagon disintegrate as it was hit by cannon fire.

Johnny heard another cannon ball whistle through the air just overhead and land with a crash in back of their position. This was followed by a bloodcurdling scream. At first Johnny

Horses killed during a battle in the Civil War.

could not identify the sound, but when he did, he felt sick all over. He knew that it was the sound of a horse in terrible agony. When the smoke cleared enough, he looked toward the place he had left his horses tethered. They were gone.

"Please," he whispered to himself. "Please let Ben and Jackie have run away. Please don't let them be. . . ." He could not bring himself to finish the sentence. He felt tears running down his face. Then he heard one of the soldiers cry out from a nearby trench, "I'm hit! I'm hit! Help me."

Johnny watched in horror as he saw another soldier climb out of the trench and scream, "Where are you? I can't find you." There was a burst of fire, and that soldier went down clutching at the place where his left arm used to be. The shouting and screams of pain filled Johnny's ears. He couldn't shut them out. Even when the firing and the explosions let up, Johnny could still hear those sounds echoing in his head.

The hours blurred together until the time when Johnny heard Captain Red shouting to his men, "This is it, boys. We have our orders. We're going after those Yankees. Invincibles, move out!"

Johnny watched the soldiers of Company C climb from the trenches and run forward. The next thing Johnny knew he was running along, right behind Roche, trying his best to keep up. Johnny didn't have a gun, but he was aware that he carried something in his right hand. It was a tree branch, and he waved it above his head. He realized that he was screaming fiercely at the top of his lungs as he charged forward with the others. The hoarse noise he made didn't sound like something that came from his own mouth. It seemed to be drawn out of him by the strange shrieks that the others were making—a chorus that would have scared even the fiercest banshees that his cousin Asa had told him about to frighten him.

As he ran, Johnny saw more horrible sights that burned themselves on his brain. He saw soldiers fall to the ground, writhing in pain. He saw a soldier trying to crawl without any legs, turning the snow red with blood. He saw a man draped over a low fence, hanging motionless where he had died. Johnny didn't want to see these things. He didn't want to look, but for some reason he stopped and stared. His stomach churned and heaved, the sourness pouring out of him onto the ground. He wished what he had seen could have been cleansed away with his vomit, but he knew these sights were etched in his mind forever.

Then Johnny heard a voice shouting, "Come on, boys! We're driving them back. The Yankees are retreating."

Johnny ran as fast as he could, but he wasn't able to keep up. He was gasping for breath, and his throat seemed to be on fire. It felt as though a sharp dagger had pierced his chest. He wondered if he, too, had been shot, but when he rubbed his hands over his chest, there was no blood, no wound. Johnny heard minié balls whistle around him. Would he get out of this alive? He started to run again as fast as he could, slipped on an icy patch in the snow, and fell, cracking his head on a rock as he went down. The last thing Johnny saw was a burst of shimmering color behind his closed eyelids. Then there was only darkness.

6

Defeat

AT LAST, THERE WERE NO MORE SOUNDS rattling about inside Johnny's head. The running and shouting, the sound of gunfire, and the booming of cannons had ended. Johnny lay suspended in a dark cave of nothingness.

Some time later Johnny moaned slightly and took a shallow breath. He tried to open his eyes, but his lids were so heavy he could not. He didn't remember where he was. Slowly he turned his aching head, first to one side and then to the other. He shivered. His feet were cold; his hands felt frozen. Why was he clutching a tree branch?

Johnny heard a familiar rhythmic thudding. He forced his eyes to open and pulled himself up on one elbow to see where the sound came from. It was a horse galloping across the snowy field.

"Ben? Jackie?" He tried to cry out, but his voice sounded pitifully weak in his own ears. "Here I am. Over here." But the horse wasn't Ben, and it wasn't Jackie. It was a horse with a saddle, but no rider. Empty stirrups flopped about as the horse ran.

Slowly Johnny began to remember what had happened. He squeezed his eyes shut and then opened them again. He saw soldiers lying all about him. Some of them were dead, their bodies already beginning to bloat. Others were alive and panting with exhaustion.

One of the soldiers struggled to his knees and cried out, "We did it, boys. We whupped 'em. We whupped 'em good this time."

Another soldier stood and called back, "You're dad-burned right, we did. We beat 'em on the river, and we beat 'em on the land."

"We showed them Yankees a thing or two," came other voices.

At least that is what the Confederate soldiers thought had happened. But, only part of it was true. The Union gunboats on the Cumberland River had been disabled and forced to leave in confusion, and the Union soldiers had been driven back in places. What the boys in butternut uniforms did not know was that they were being surrounded by reinforcements. More Yankees!

Johnny managed to stand up and walk although he had no sense of which direction to go. He had become separated from Roche during the battle, and he straggled along beside men he didn't recognize. Johnny was mightily thirsty, but on the trampled ground there was only muddy water to drink. He scooped up a handful of dirty snow and sucked on it. He stumbled over the hilly terrain across which he had been running only a few hours earlier.

He strained his eyes looking for a familiar face. As if in a dream, Johnny thought he recognized the Kentucky soldier and his dog, Frank, who walked close to his master's side. Johnny closed his eyes and shook his head to try to clear the muzzy feeling that made him question what he saw. When he opened his eyes again, the Kentucky man and the dog were nowhere in sight.

There was no sign of any soldiers from the 4th Mississippi either. Johnny moved in what he hoped was the direction of the place where the Mississippi trenches had been. He squinted as he tried to see through the trees, searching for his horses and wagon. Then he remembered that the wagon had been destroyed. He could only hope that Ben and Jackie had somehow made it through the battle.

Johnny's legs were weak and felt spongy, as though they would not support his body. At last, he could go on no longer. He sank down and leaned against a shattered tree, the world around him a blur of misery. Johnny was so weary that he closed his eyes and welcomed the comforting darkness that flowed over him.

The Confederate generals argued late into the night about their situation. The men in charge decided against trying to cut their way through the Union lines that had them encircled. Two of those generals, John B. Floyd and Gideon J. Pillow, managed to slip away from Fort Donelson, getting some of their troops across the Cumberland.

They left a third officer, General Simon B. Buckner, to do the unpleasant work of surrendering. The next day, General Buckner prepared a white flag of truce to send to Union General Ulysses S. Grant. The Confederate soldiers, including those of the 4th Mississippi, were ordered back to their trenches. The soldiers were numb from cold, hunger, and disbelief. They slogged angrily back over ground they thought they had won. A fierce glowing rage was building up inside of them as they returned to the rifle pits from which they had come.

When he opened his eyes once more, Johnny was surprised to see that he was sitting on the ground next to a tree. The sun shone brightly on the snow. Johnny heard soldiers on all sides of him cursing generals Floyd and Pillow, the leaders who had betrayed them. Many of the soldiers were plagued by the shame of Fort Henry all over again. Johnny heard another sound, but it was faint, and he had to strain to listen. It was music, but where was it coming from? What did it mean? Johnny summoned every bit of strength he had and struggled to his feet. He stumbled toward the distant, quavering sound.

Johnny squinted into the bright sunlight trying to make sense of the motion he saw in the distance. He rubbed his eyes, not sure that he was really seeing what he thought he saw. There were hundreds—no, thousands—of soldiers coming steadily across the low hills and valleys. Line upon line of soldiers. Their feet crunched rhythmically over the icy ground. These soldiers were not wearing the grayish-brown uniforms of the Confederacy that had become familiar to Johnny. They were dressed in Union blue. Sunlight glinted from the rifles on their shoulders. Johnny saw the red, white, and blue of the United States flag fluttering proudly in their midst. He also saw other flags of red, blue, gold, and green, their regimental colors. Above the noise of the soldiers' tramping feet, Johnny could hear a melody. A band was playing "Yankee Doodle."

Johnny stopped to stare as he saw more Union soldiers. They were rounding up Confederate soldiers and directing them to stack their muskets in surrender. Johnny fell in with them, and they were ordered to march to the river near the small town of Dover. As he marched, Johnny listened to what was being said by one of the Confederate soldiers nearest to him.

"Capture of Fort Donelson—Charge of the Eighth Missouri Regiment and the Eleventh Indiana Zouaves, February 15th, 1862."

"We'll be going home soon, boys. All we have to do is take the oath of allegiance, promising that we'll not fight the Yankees anymore. Then, they'll give us all paroles." Johnny's heart thumped excitedly inside his chest. If the Confederate soldiers were allowed to go home, he would certainly be able to go back to his family. The veteran soldiers knew that was the way it had been after other battles. Soldiers on the losing side were paroled and allowed to go home. They thought for certain it would be that way this time, too. But, they were wrong.

Following the Battle of Fort Donelson, General Grant was given a new nickname by newspaper reporters. From then on,

A casualty of the Civil War.

his initials, U. S., would stand for *Unconditional Surrender* Grant. That was because this was what he demanded of the Southern troops.

General Buckner was outraged. He had sent a white flag to General Grant, saying he would be willing to meet and discuss the terms of surrender. Buckner had expected, as did the soldiers, that these terms would mean the soldiers would be free to go. Grant, however, had different ideas. Unconditional surrender meant that this time there would be no paroles offered.

Grant knew what had happened in the past, after other battles. Enemy soldiers had promised not to return to fight again. Once they got home, however, many of these paroled men re-enlisted. Sometimes they joined up again because of a deep belief in the correctness of their cause. Others were forced to go back into the army by recruiters. General Grant did not want these 12,000 Confederate prisoners to return to their ranks and fight against the Union. That would just prolong the war. So, this time there would be no paroles for prisoners.

The Battle of Fort Donelson may have been over, but the Confederate soldiers were not allowed to go free. Instead of going home, Johnny was lined up along with the Rebel soldiers. They were all going north as prisoners of war. The Southern soldiers could not believe what they had heard. It wasn't fair. It was particularly hard for Johnny to understand. He was going to be sent even farther from his home in Kentucky, and there was nothing he could do about it.

Herded North

THE BITTERLY FRIGID WEATHER and gnawing hunger continued. Johnny and the other prisoners stood in mud so deep it was over the tops of their shoes. Johnny was more miserable than he had ever felt before. It was strange how the cold made his fingers seem to burn as though they were on fire and his feet so numb he could not even feel his toes.

Johnny found himself in the midst of hundreds of persons, not one of whom he knew. He had never felt so alone in his life. His head was spinning with dizziness, but he managed to make his way over to where some Union guards were standing. One of the soldiers pointed his rifle at Johnny.

"You'd best get back in line, Reb."

"You don't understand," Johnny tried to tell him. "I'm not a soldier. This is all a mistake. I just want to go home."

"We all want to go home," the guard said. "Now, get back where you belong."

"What did that boy say?" another guard asked his comrade.

"He said that he wasn't a soldier," the first guard replied.

"Well, he does look kind of puny," the soldier said, and both men laughed.

As Johnny turned away from the Union guards, he felt someone grab his arm.

"Sprout, is that you? We thought we'd lost you for sure."

Johnny stared at the dirty face of the man who had taken hold of him. It took a minute for him to realize that the voice belonged to Dudley Wallace of Company C.

"Come on," said Wallace. "We're over here."

Wallace guided Johnny through the crowd of prisoners. Then Johnny saw other men he recognized. There were Hector Hamilton, William Cade, and Johnny Roche. Roche's face was as grimy as Wallace's, and Johnny thought it was tear-streaked. An expression that might have been a smile flickered across Roche's face as he greeted Johnny Ables. The two Johnnys stood leaning on each other for support and warmth as they waited.

The prisoners didn't really know what they were waiting for. They wondered what would happen to them next. It seemed as though it took forever before they were told anything. When they did hear, it was frightening news. They were to be put on boats and sent downriver to a Northern prison camp.

It was almost ten o'clock at night when they were lined up and marched to the dock in the little town of Dover. Johnny saw a steamboat lying at anchor in the Cumberland River. The name on the side of the boat was the *Empress*.

Johnny was asleep on his feet as he waited with the others to get onto the boat. The guards searched each prisoner.

A "group of Confederate prisoners captured at Fort Donelson on the morning after the surrender."

"What are they looking for?" Johnny asked.

"They're hunting for hidden weapons," Wallace said. "They are taking any pistols or knives that someone may have under his shirt or in his pant leg."

"I saw them take one feller's little ole pen knife," Hamilton said. "It wasn't big enough to stick a flea with."

"Don't seem fair. They let the officers keep their sidearms," said Cade.

A soldier standing nearby said, "I heard that Commander Drake was mad as a wet hen, and he busted his sword over his knee and threw both pieces in the river."

When it finally came his turn, Johnny shuffled along with the rest of the prisoners who were herded up the gang-plank onto the jam-packed decks of the boat. Once aboard,

Johnny could hardly move, it was so crowded. He was squeezed between Roche, Cade, and Hamilton with scarcely room to take a breath.

"Well, there's one good thing about being huddled up like this," Hamilton said, "It cuts that bitter wind, so we're not as cold as we might be."

Johnny's belly growled with emptiness. He couldn't remember when he'd last had anything to eat. There was no place for him or any of the other prisoners to sit or lie down. They were all wet and muddy and miserable. To make matters worse, many of the prisoners were ill. Some of them coughed until they vomited. Others had stomach upsets or diarrhea. There was no place for them to relieve themselves except on the crowded decks. Johnny clamped one hand over his nose, trying to shut out the odor, but it was overpowering. He felt his stomach begin to heave.

Army transport Bridgeport. *This is the type of steamboat that was used to transport Confederate soldiers to prison camps during the Civil War.*

Johnny heard some of the other soldiers talking among themselves.

"Where do you suppose they're taking us?"

"What do you think the prison camp will be like?"

"How are the Yankees going to treat us when we get there?"

Some of the men admitted to their comrades that besides being hungry and sick, they were afraid, too. The voices in the darkness seemed to echo the very thoughts that were in Johnny's mind. Fear of the unknown seemed to hover over everyone like a dark storm cloud.

All of a sudden, Johnny was startled as the boat's whistle sounded a shrill blast, and the *Empress* began to churn its way sluggishly down the river. He was so tired he could not bear to stand any longer. Even though he was afraid of being trampled by the feet of the prisoners who were packed tightly together, he let himself sink down on the filthy deck.

It was a wretched, slow journey. Johnny closed his eyes and drifted into a state of half sleep, half wakefulness. Once when he inhaled, he thought he smelled the steamy aroma rising from a pot of rabbit stew, the thick gravy afloat with chunks of potato. Just as he lifted a spoonful to his mouth, he awakened, licking his dry, cracked lips with disappointment. His stomach was still a vast, empty cave. The only fragrance that filled his nostrils was that of the sick, stinking men who pressed against him.

Johnny closed his eyes again, and this time he dreamed that he stood in front of a crackling fire so hot that it singed the

58

Captured! A Boy Trapped in the Civil War

hair on his arms as he stretched his hands towards it. When he awakened a second time, he was still shivering with a cold so deep it seemed to freeze his aching innards.

His tired mind drifted back into sleep once more. This time he dreamed of his mother in their little house in Calloway County. He reached out to touch the softness of her cheeks as she brushed his sisters' shining hair. He awakened with a wrenching homesickness that was worse than either hunger or cold.

Johnny had no way to keep track of the hours that passed. When the boat stopped at last, he knew only that they had passed through another period of light, and now it was dark again. When daylight came once more, Johnny managed to get to his feet and saw that the boat was near the shore of a large town.

"That's Cairo, Illinois," he heard someone say. This information was passed along until it circled the boat and came back again like an echo.

"Maybe this is where we'll be in prison," another soldier said.

Johnny waited, but nothing seemed to be happening. The boat stayed where it was in the water. No one came to tell the prisoners what to do. They waited and wondered. Those who were closest to the railings of the boat could see large chunks of ice floating in the water.

The sun finally put in an appearance and warmed those persons who were lucky enough to be standing near a rail. In a powerful surge the prisoners nearest Johnny started to push in that direction. They were making a desperate attempt to find a place in the sunshine, and Johnny felt himself being shoved and dragged along. Suddenly, he could feel the boat tip to one side.

"Get back! Get back!" one of the Union guards shouted gruffly. The other guards joined in the chant and used their rifle barrels to try to force the freezing prisoners to move away from the railing. If the boat tipped much more, there was danger that river water would get into the steam boilers that powered the vessel.

"Do you want this boat to explode and kill us all?" another of the guards cried frantically. The suffering men paid no attention to the attempts to move them back. They did not seem to care any longer what happened to them. That pitiful bit of warmth from the pale sun was all that seemed important to them at the moment.

Another day passed by, and the prisoners were still kept onboard the boat. "What are they waiting for?" one prisoner anxiously asked another.

The reply was not comforting, "Maybe they are going to keep us here. Maybe this boat is going to be our prison."

The guards didn't know any more than the prisoners did about their fate. Johnny thought they seemed every bit as unhappy as the men they were guarding. The Union soldiers were cold and hungry and tired, too. Johnny sensed this was a dangerous situation.

As it turned out, the waiting was for another steamboat that was transporting more captured Confederate soldiers.

They would travel on together. Finally, the guards ordered the prisoners to move down the gangplanks. They were going to leave the boat at last. Once on land, the Union soldiers herded the prisoners onto trains. The lucky ones who were first in line were put on passenger cars with seats. When the seats were full and the aisles packed with people, the rest of the prisoners were loaded onto freight cars.

Johnny heard all sorts of rumors circulating about where they were going to be sent. By now, however, he had reached the point where he did not really care. One place up North would be the same as any other to him. All he knew was that he was being taken farther away from Calloway County, Kentucky. He didn't know if he would ever see his mother and his little sisters again.

Johnny leaned back in the seat and closed his eyes. Sleep was the only escape he could find. He took a deep breath as he began to drift off into another dream about food. He could smell a wonderful aroma, but this time it was not a dream. It was real. Johnny smelled real food and steaming hot coffee. The famished prisoners managed to make room in the crowded aisles for women who were handing out food and drink.

"They're Catholic nuns called the Sisters of Charity," someone whispered. Johnny thought they looked like angels.

The starving men quickly gobbled the food, but it was too much for stomachs that had been so long without anything to eat. It made them nauseated, and many of the men were sick again.

The train began to roll and so did the rumors.

A Map of Johnny's Journey

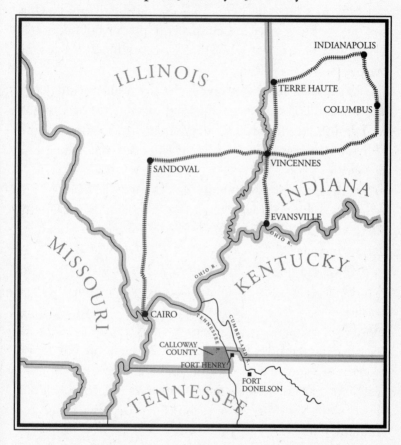

This map shows where Johnny Ables's family lived in Calloway County, Kentucky; where the 4th Mississippi Infantry Regiment fought at Fort Henry on the Tennessee River in Tennessee; where Johnny and the Red Invincibles were engaged in battle at Fort Donelson on the Cumberland River in Tennessee; the steamboat route that Johnny and the Confederate prisoners took down the Cumberland River from Fort Donelson to the Ohio River and down the Ohio River to Cairo, Illinois; the train route north from Cairo to Sandoval, Illinois, and east from Sandoval to Vincennes, Indiana; and the two possible train routes from Vincennes to Indianapolis.

"We're going to be sent to one camp, but our officers will be going to a different place." This rumor proved to be true, but no one knew to which camp any of them would be going. There were prisoner-of-war camps set up in Illinois, Ohio, and even as far away as New York.

As the train picked up speed, the rhythmic clacking of its wheels on the metal rails seemed to beat time to the thoughts in Johnny's head. Farther from home. Farther from home. Wherever he was going, every clickety-clack was taking him farther from home.

As the sky lightened, Johnny looked out of the window. The train was rolling through countryside unfamiliar to Johnny. Then he heard one of the prisoners say, "I used to live up here. This is Indiana."

When the train finally came to a stop, it was dark again. Word was passed along from prisoner to prisoner that they had reached a city called Indianapolis. Indianapolis was nothing more than a strange name to Johnny's ears. It didn't really matter where he was now. He was so tired, all he wanted to do was to get warm and go to sleep. Instead, he was nudged out of the seat. Once again, Johnny numbly obeyed orders. He moved slowly along with the rest of the prisoners as they were herded from the train.

"You are going to bed down here in the station freight house tonight," a guard told the prisoners. "Tomorrow you will be going to Camp Morton."

Johnny saw the guards carrying large wash tubs filled with coffee into the station. The prisoners lined up to get a cup of the steaming hot liquid. The first gulp of coffee burned Johnny's tongue, but it helped warm him. He took the bakery bread and some boiled beef that was offered to him. He had learned his lesson earlier about eating too quickly. This time, he took only small bites and chewed slowly, testing to see if his stomach was ready to accept the food.

Johnny heard one of the prisoners grumbling, "This meat is only half-cooked." Several others voiced their agreement, but Johnny noticed that no matter how bad they said the food was, the men ate it anyway.

There were no beds in the freight house, nor were there any blankets. The only place for the prisoners to sleep was on the floor. Johnny wiggled around trying to get comfortable. As he closed his eyes, the last thing he saw was the guards with their guns, watching him and the other prisoners. As miserable and frightened as he was, Johnny was so tired that sleep came quickly. He hardly had time to wonder what awaited him the next day.

8

"Heads up. Step Smartly."

THE NEXT MORNING, the Union guards instructed the prisoners to line up. They were told that they were going to march from the freight house, where they had spent the night, to a place called Camp Morton. It was a little over a mile away.

Johnny, like the others, did what he was told. He had learned that when a person was tired, cold, and unhappy, it was easier to put one foot in front of the other without thinking. At times he felt as though he were sleepwalking.

"Looks like we're going to have to run the gauntlet again," complained one of the prisoners. "Just like we did at Fort Donelson."

Johnny did not know what a gauntlet was. Cade explained to him. "Take a look around, and you'll see what it means."

At Fort Donelson the Confederate soldiers, because they were the defeated enemy, had to march between long lines of Union soldiers. Here in Indianapolis, there were jostling crowds waiting outside the railroad station and lined up on both sides of the street. Johnny thought there might be hundreds of them. In fact, there were thousands. The onlookers here, however, were not soldiers. They were curious Northern townspeople who had come to stare at the battle-weary prisoners being paraded in their midst.

There were people of all ages in the crowd, and they were all outfitted in their Sunday-go-to-meeting best. Women wore fancy bonnets adorned with nets and feathers, tied under their chins with wide ribbons. Their heavy capes had fur trim at the collars. The men wore warm-looking coats and sported tall black silk hats. The children, with well-scrubbed faces, were dressed in the grand style of their parents.

"Blasted Yanks," grumbled another prisoner. "They've turned out to enjoy the show."

At first, Johnny wondered what show the prisoner was talking about. Then he realized that he and the other prisoners were part of that show. He felt as though he were some strange animal being exhibited at a circus.

"So that's what the 'Secesh' look like," said a man in the crowd of Northerners.

"They're a ragtag bunch," another said.

Johnny was well aware what the prisoners must look like to these people. He could see Hamilton and Cade, their faces and hands still grimy from the smoke of the battlefield. There had been no way for them to wash themselves in many days. Their clothing was caked with mud and tattered from hard use during the fighting and the journey north. Johnny realized

Sumner Cunningham of the 41st Tennessee Infantry encouraged the first prisoners at Camp Morton to march into the prison with dignity.

with shock that he must look every bit as disheveled as did Hamilton, Cade, and all of the others. He ducked his head in shame. He was glad his ma could not see him now. She always said, "We may not have nice things like a lot of other folks, but we can always be neat and clean."

"Come on, boys," called out one of the other prisoners, who was striding along, looking as though he were proud to be in this parade. "Heads up. Step smartly. Shoulders squared."

"Who is that feller?" someone wanted to know.

"He's a Tennessean named Sumner Archibald Cunningham. That boy is going to make his mark in the world someday."

"Remember who we are," Cunningham said, as he proudly called out the name of his company: "We are the Richmond Gentries."

"Cunningham is right," said Cade. "Let's show these Hoosiers what real soldiers look like. Chins up. We're the Red Invincibles."

Other prisoners, some barely able to hobble along, took up the challenge to march with pride. They tried to recall those days long ago when they left home with their new battle flags flying proudly. The sound of drums and bugles were summoned up in their memories. Those were the days when they thought the war was going to be a glorious adventure. They almost expected the pretty girls in the crowd to rush out and kiss them.

"We're the Stephens Guard," a prisoner from Company E of the 4th Mississippi called out.

"We're the Carroll County Rebels," said another.

One by one, companies announced themselves as the "Sons of the South," the "Benela Sharpshooters," and the "Nelson Grays."

A group of ragtag Confederate prisoners.

Johnny noticed that Williams was having a hard time of it. He could walk only with the aid of two other prisoners. Johnny recalled how ill Williams had been that day he had ridden on Johnny's wagon as they headed toward Fort Donelson. He felt proud of Williams for managing to hold his head up a bit higher as he hobbled along.

Although Johnny wasn't really one of the Red Invincibles, he squared his shoulders and thrust out his chin. He was determined to stare all those gawking folks directly in their eyes. There wasn't much else he could do about his situation. At least, he wasn't going to let them make him feel ashamed.

Surprisingly, he did feel better once he stopped ducking his head, hoping no one would notice him.

The Union guard had told them the prison camp was only a little over a mile from the railroad station. It seemed to Johnny that he had marched three times that far in uncomfortable shoes that were soggy with snow and mud from the battlefield.

It was late afternoon when the prisoners arrived at the main gate of the prison. Johnny looked up as he went through the opening and noticed that the top of the gate had been made to look like a draped curtain with tassel-like decorations. The words "MILITARY PRISON: CAMP MORTON" were emblazoned across the top. At each side was a thick post topped by a structure that looked like a birdhouse to Johnny. The whitewashed fence that surrounded the camp was as high as two tall men, one standing on the other's shoulders, and was constructed of wide oak planks fitted closely together.

Johnny could see Union sentries with rifles as they patrolled along an outside wooden walkway that was built about four feet below the top of the wall. To his discouraged eyes, it seemed that escape from this place would be impossible.

Once inside, the prisoners looked around to see what their prison camp was like. Camp Morton covered a large area of land. One of the soldiers who had been a farmer back in Mississippi looked at it with a practiced eye and reckoned that it was about thirty-five acres. He was close; it was actually thirty-six. There were lofty bare walnut and oak trees on the grounds, which were every bit as muddy as the battlefields had been.

There was also a stream named "State Ditch" that ran through the entire width of the camp. Later, the prisoners would rename this ditch "The Potomac."

Johnny saw many buildings on the prison grounds, but the one that would be of special interest to him was a long peaked-roof building on the other side of the stream. This would be his barracks, a roughly made building with gaps between the wooden boards on the sides that let cold air rush in.

"These look like old cow sheds to me," Roche said.

Roche was right. These buildings had been stalls where livestock were kept not so long ago. Camp Morton was located on what had been the grounds of the Indiana State Fair. When the war started, it was turned into a training camp for Union soldiers. Now it was to be used as a prisoner-of-war camp. Both the inside and outside of the animal stalls had been whitewashed.

It had been an impossible job to find enough room to take care of nearly four thousand prisoners of war on short notice. Even the cattle stalls did not provide enough room for the large number of Southern soldiers that was supposed to be sent to Camp Morton after the Battle of Fort Donelson. Other Indiana towns volunteered to take care of their share of men. About fifteen hundred prisoners were sent on to Lafayette and Terre Haute until more barracks could be built in Indianapolis. Johnny stared at the place where he would live until. . . . He could not bring himself to finish this thought because he had no idea how long he would be here. Johnny couldn't bear to imagine what the future might bring. He dared not let himself think about getting out of this place and going home.

The guards were told to keep each regiment together in the prison barracks. The men of Company C were happy to meet up again with friends from the other companies of the 4th Mississippi even though the quarters were crowded. Johnny's bed was one of the bunks that lined the walls on both sides of the building. The people of Indianapolis had donated straw to make the wooden boards a bit softer. Other people had given blankets for the prisoners to use. It was far more comfortable than anything he had experienced in a long time. Johnny was so tired, he sat down gratefully on the planks.

The next morning, all the prisoners lined up by company on the parade ground. Union guards wrote down each prisoner's name on a sheet of paper. When it came Johnny's turn to be enrolled, he stepped forward.

"What is your name and rank?" The guard wanted to know.

Johnny replied, "I am not a soldier. I'm not supposed to be a prisoner here."

The guard looked at him and shook his head. "I can't do anything about that. Now, just tell me your name."

Cade stepped forward and said, "The boy is telling the truth. He's not a soldier. We made him come with us so he could cut wood."

Again the soldier shook his head. "I'm not in charge here. I have to do what I'm told, and my orders are to register every prisoner. Now, don't cause any trouble. Tell me your name."

Johnny sighed. He sensed that it would not be wise for him to cause any difficulty on his first day at Camp Morton. "My name is Ables. John Ables."

The soldier wrote, "Ab*els*, John."

Rations were issued for that day, and once again the men gobbled this food as though they were ravenous wolves. They would learn later not to eat all their rations at once but to save some of it for later in the day. They would also learn to keep anything they saved in their haversacks and to keep those haversacks with them at all times. Hunger does strange things to human beings. There were some prisoners who would steal food from their own comrades if it was not closely guarded.

If there was anything positive about Camp Morton it was that there was a supply of good water for the prisoners to drink. They were able to heat it so that they could use it for washing themselves and their filthy clothing. The bad thing about washing their clothes was that there was nowhere to hang them outside, and it was so cold, they would not have dried outside anyway. When damp clothing was hung inside the barracks, it made the place even more dank and uncomfortable for the prisoners.

It was an unusually cold winter, even for Indiana. For Southerners who were unused to this kind of weather, it was especially hard. Many of the prisoners caught colds, and this often developed into pneumonia.

There wasn't much for the prisoners to do to entertain themselves. They spent most of their time in or near their cow-barn barracks. A lot of the men spent the time reading the Bibles they had been given when they became soldiers. Preachers from the town were allowed to come inside the prison camp and hold church meetings.

Some of the more adventurous prisoners visited other parts of the camp, even though they were not supposed to do this. The guards had been ordered to separate the different regiments. There were always fellows, however, who managed to break the rules and get away with it.

Mostly, the prisoners passed the long, boring hours by talking. Some of the boys could tell a good story and make everyone laugh. Laughter was needed at a time like this. One Tennessee boy told about what happened to a friend of his during the Battle of Fort Donelson. The soldier, whose name was Ben Loftin, was so tired that when there was a lull in the fighting, he sat down on the icy ground to rest. He leaned against the wheel of a gun carriage and fell asleep. Suddenly, the cannon was fired and when it went off, Ben jumped up quickly. His trousers, however, were frozen to the ground and stayed put when Ben moved. Ben had to find another pair to wear. He refused to say exactly where he had "borrowed" them.

Johnny liked another funny story that made the rounds. It seemed that some fellow from Indianapolis was so curious about the prisoners that he decided to get a close-up look at them. As the prisoners marched down the street, this fellow fell into line and marched right along as though he were one of them. In fact, he marched with them right through the prison gates and into Camp Morton. When he tried to leave, the Union soldiers who were guarding the gates would not let him out. The fellow flew into a rage at being kept inside with the Rebels. When rations were handed out, he refused to take them. He didn't want to eat those rations because he was not a prisoner. He finally had to spend a long hungry night sharing a bunk with a Secesh.

"Good enough for him," said one of the prisoners.

"But too bad for the Secesh who had to share a bed with him," another prisoner roared with laughter.

That foolish fellow wasn't freed until the next day when he managed to find someone with enough influence to get him out of Camp Morton.

Johnny and Roche were delighted when, once again, they saw the little dog called Frank. He was still with his master, the soldier from the 2nd Kentucky, who had also been taken prisoner and brought to Camp Morton. The two of them made the rounds, and Frank ate whatever scraps of food the prisoners shared with him.

One day some Union guards tried to lure Frank away with juicier morsels of food than the prisoners could provide. Frank, however, simply looked at the guards in much the same teasing way he had looked at Roche and Johnny that day they first met him in the Tennessee woods. No matter how the guards pleaded, the dog obediently returned to his master.

As days passed, life in prison camp began to seem like some strange dream to Johnny. Some mornings when he awakened in his bunk, he had the feeling that he was back at home in his own bed. For a few moments, before he opened his eyes, he would think that none of this had happened. Then he would wake fully and realize, with a terrible sinking feeling in the pit of his stomach, that he was still in prison. The battle, the trip north, and Camp Morton were real. This was not a horrible nightmare from which he would awaken.

9

Prison Life

JOHNNY ABLES MAY NOT HAVE REALIZED it when he first arrived in Indianapolis, but a man named Richard Owen was going to play a very important part in his life during the next few weeks. In fact, Owen would play a memorable part in the lives of all of the original prisoners at Camp Morton.

The prisoners began, right away, to keep a close eye on the slender man who made daily rounds of the camp. Johnny noticed that he paused occasionally to speak with some of them. Although he wore the blue uniform of an officer in the Union army, he appeared to be more like a kindly pastor calling on members of his church. He was, however, the commandant of this prison camp, and he held the well-being of thousands of prisoners in his hands.

The Confederate soldiers immediately started to ask questions about Colonel Owen. They wanted to find out what kind of a person he really was. Bit by bit they managed to put together the picture of a most unusual man.

"The colonel lived down South for a long time," Wallace said. Someone had told him that Owen, at one time, was a teacher at the Western Military Institute in Kentucky. Owen later became part owner of that school. When the school moved to Nashville, Tennessee, Owen went there to live.

"If he lived in the South, maybe he understands what it is we are fighting for," Cade said.

"There's no doubt that he understands. He's a right smart fellow," Wallace agreed. "But that doesn't mean he goes along with Southern views. I heard he took a strong stand against slavery when he was down South."

Cade seemed disappointed by this. Hamilton added his bit, "Some of the Kentucky fellers were saying that in spite of those opinions, Owen was still popular with his Southern students."

Little by little, their knowledge of Colonel Richard Owen grew as the prisoners gathered more tidbits of information about him and put them together. One of the prisoners said he heard that at one time, Owen had studied medicine. That was true. Somebody else shared the information that Owen had been a soldier in an earlier war. That was true also. Owen was an army captain in 1847 and 1848 during the Mexican War.

After living in the South for several years, Owen finally decided that it would be best for him to return to the family home in Indiana. Once back there, Owen went to work for his brother, David Dale Owen, who was the Indiana state geologist. Together they were hired to survey the central part of the state. When his brother died two years later, Richard Owen was appointed state geologist in his brother's place. He was busy working as a surveyor when the war between the Northern and Southern states began.

A photograph of Colonel Richard Owen, first commandant of Camp Morton Prison, taken many years after the end of the Civil War.

Owen enlisted in the Union army right away and recruited a regiment of soldiers. Early in the war, Colonel Owen led his soldiers in several battles. Indiana Governor Oliver Morton, for whom the prison was named, called upon Owen to become the commandant of Camp Morton.

Colonel Owen came from a well-known family. The Owens moved to the United States from Scotland. The colonel's father was Robert Owen, who was the leader of a community in southern Indiana called New Harmony. This community was dedicated to creating a place where people could live together peacefully. All the members of New Harmony were supposed to work together for the good of the community. Fortunately for the prisoners from Fort Donelson, Owen followed his father's example. Seeking the good of everyone was the way Colonel Owen decided to operate Camp Morton.

Owen organized the prison camp in such a way that the prisoners' own first sergeants were allowed to be in charge of their men and see that they behaved in an orderly manner. The first sergeants would act as a court of appeal to hear cases of misbehavior and pass fair judgment when discipline was needed. The colonel hoped that this would create a positive atmosphere and prevent the prisoners from becoming restless and causing trouble.

This did not mean that there were no problems or that life was easy at Camp Morton. It was, after all, a prison camp. Colonel Owen had strict rules and made sure the prisoners followed them. He didn't want anyone trying to escape. Each morning every prisoner who was able had to assemble for roll call. The prisoners were guarded by Union soldiers, although most of these guards were untrained for such duty. Some guards were easy on the prisoners, while others were too strict. Johnny and the prisoners were warned that they must not make insulting remarks to the guards. He also knew that the guards were

Guards at Camp Morton Prison in Indianapolis, Indiana, during the Civil War.

not supposed to talk to the prisoners, but he noticed that it was hard to make either of those rules stick.

The Southerners imprisoned at Camp Morton had a major cause for unhappiness: they did not like the food they were given. This was a common complaint of soldiers in every war. Even the Union soldiers stationed at Camp Morton wrote letters home telling how much they disliked the food. The Confederates were now eating the same kind of rations that the Northern soldiers had been given when they were stationed at this place. For men who had been starving only a few days earlier, it seemed a strange thing to complain about; nevertheless, complain they did.

Many of the Southern soldiers griped that Northern bacon had too much fat in it. Some said it was too salty; others said it wasn't salty enough. Johnny heard one prisoner complain that there wasn't enough drippings with the meat. He could agree with that since he liked a bit of gravy to dip his bread in.

There were lots of other complaints.

"The dried apples are wormy."

"The beans aren't any good."

"The coffee don't taste right." It certainly didn't taste anything like the coffee the prisoners had been drinking. They liked coffee with the strong flavor of the ground root of the chicory plant. That is what they had used instead of coffee during the hard times of the war.

A great many of the prisoners didn't like the bakery bread they were given. "It sure would be good to have some corn bread like we eat back home," one homesick prisoner complained. When Johnny heard comments like that, it made him long for his ma's good cooking.

Colonel Owen, himself, listened to the prisoners and tried his best to have the menu adjusted. He had to consider money, however. He could not always afford to give the prisoners everything they wanted. In spite of their complaints about the food, Johnny noticed that the prisoners made sure they got their daily allotment.

One morning, Johnny heard shouting. He and his comrades hurried to see what the cause of the excitement was. They saw one of the Confederate sergeants who was in charge of handing out the food arguing with a prisoner.

"You ain't being fair. You gave him more than you gave me," the prisoner accused.

"You got all that was coming to you," the sergeant said as he started to move on.

The unhappy prisoner followed the sergeant, taunting him, "How come you give some folks more than others get? You think they're somebody special? They giving you some reason to cheat us?"

The sergeant picked up a stick of firewood and jabbed his accuser with it. The man grabbed a club and lunged at the sergeant, knocking him to the ground. Before guards could get there to stop the fight, the angry prisoner stood over the downed sergeant, hitting him again and again and again. Johnny was sickened by this vicious attack. He felt even worse when he learned that the Confederate sergeant died a few hours later.

Occasionally, there was more pleasant activity. One day as Johnny lay on his bunk, he heard Roche calling to him, "Get up. Come with me." Johnny wanted to know where they were going.

"Hurry up, or we'll be too late. They're handing out mattresses," Roche said as he began running in the direction of the gate. Roche elbowed his way through the crowd of men who had gathered around a large wagon. Johnny followed Roche as he had done so often. Some women in Indianapolis had made ninety-three soft feather mattresses and had them delivered to Camp Morton. Roche managed to grab one of them, but Johnny wasn't so lucky.

"It's all right," Roche assured him. "We'll take turns with this one. I'll sleep on it one night, and you can have it the next."

The people of Indianapolis were of differing opinions about how the prisoners should be treated. There were generous persons, like the ladies who donated the mattresses. They felt sorry for the prisoners and gave them a variety of things to help improve their lives. Some kind individuals gave money for the prisoners. Colonel Owen saw to it that this money was carefully divided and given to the prisoners as a regular allowance. This made it possible for them to purchase tobacco, newspapers, magazines, and postage stamps from the sutlers who were allowed to come into camp.

Colonel Owen encouraged people, especially his friends from the New Harmony community, to donate books to the prison. Owen thought that reading would help the prisoners pass the time and make them more contented.

On the other hand, there were those persons who thought that Colonel Owen was being too easy on the Rebs. They complained publicly, saying that people who helped the prisoners were Southern sympathizers. Newspapers printed some of these complaints criticizing the good colonel. Some Indianapolis citizens were upset that prisoners were allowed to leave the camp so that they could visit their comrades in the hospital. It didn't help matters when some of the prisoners took advantage of this privilege. On their way back to camp, they stopped at a local pub. After drinking too much, they created quite a ruckus in the streets.

As it turned out, a great many of the prisoners were ill, and the number was growing daily. When they arrived at Camp Morton, there were some forty or fifty who needed to be in a hospital. Two days later, the number had grown to one hundred. By March 3, 1862, that number had doubled. Many Indianapolis women volunteered to act as nurses at the hospital. Even though it was against government rules, some private families took sick prisoners into their homes to care for them.

Some of the Company C boys went to visit Williams, who was in the hospital. When they returned, their report on his condition was not hopeful. There was more gloom among the 4th Mississippi soldiers when word came that the first few prisoners to die were comrades from their regiment.

Johnny, himself, was not feeling at all well. He spent a lot of time lying on his bunk wrapped in a cover, trying to keep warm. He tried not to think about the prisoners who had died in a Northern prison hospital so far from home. Roche did everything he could to boost Johnny's spirits.

One morning, Roche had some good news to tell Johnny. "I heard that Colonel Owen is going to let us receive letters. Not only that, we're going to be allowed to write letters home." That was the good part. The bad news was that the length of these letters was limited to only one page. If a letter was too long, it was burned. All the letters that the prisoners received or wrote were inspected by the camp postmaster before they were mailed. A few of those letters got into the hands of Union soldiers who passed along amusing stories about some of the more interesting messages.

Cade was mighty unhappy when he heard that there was some story going around about a letter he had received from home. "Who gave them the right to look at private words written to me by my wife?"

Some of the prisoners had received packages from home. These were opened by the guards to make sure no one had mailed weapons to the soldiers to be used in an uprising. Roche laughed heartily as he reported to Johnny about one package that caused quite an uproar among the guards. This particular gift was not dangerous to anyone except that it caused some hurt feelings on the part of the prisoner who received it.

"What was in the package?" Johnny wanted to know.

"It was a pair of fancy embroidered slippers," Roche said. "They sure aren't going to be much use to him in all this mud."

Johnny and Roche weren't the only ones who got a laugh out of this incident. The prisoner who received the useless gift had to endure taunts such as, "When we have our fancy dance party, can I borrow your new slippers?"

Hamilton received a box full of jams and jellies. The men in Company C were delighted, as they were sure that Hamilton would share some of it with them. The expectation of these tasty morsels soon turned to bitterness when it was learned that all such delicacies were to be given to the men who were in the hospital.

Hamilton mourned his loss for days. "I feel mighty sorry for those fellers in the hospital, but it seems like I deserved to have at least one taste of my own blackberry preserves." Johnny could understand Hamilton's disappointment. He thought about the preserves his ma used to make after he and his little sisters had picked berries in the woods. They would eat more than they brought home, but there would still be plenty to make preserves, even after his ma had made a couple of pies.

Yes, Johnny, like Hamilton, would have given almost anything for a bite of sweet fruit jam.

When Johnny learned that the prisoners were allowed to write letters home, he saved the little bit of money he had been given out of the camp fund. He would use it to buy paper and stamps. Now he had a way to let his ma and little sisters know where he was.

It was difficult for Johnny to write his letter. He puzzled long and hard about just what he should tell them. He didn't want them to worry about him. He decided he wouldn't tell them about how cold and hungry and scared he had been. Neither would he tell them about the cough that kept him awake much of the night. He would not write of the bad dreams he had when he was finally able to sleep.

He wrote, "I am at a place called Camp Morton in Indianapolis. Colonel Owen, who runs the camp, is a kind man and tries to take good care of us. They give us enough to eat here." He didn't say that more often than not, his stomach churned and heaved right after he had eaten. Instead he wrote, "No matter what they give us, it's not as good as what you cook. I surely do miss eating at home."

Johnny gnawed on the pen in his hand trying to think of something else to say. Finally he wrote, "I have made lots of new friends here. Most of them are from Mississippi. My best friend is Johnny Roche."

Then he remembered Frank and thought his sisters would enjoy knowing about that. "There is a dog here in camp with us. He makes us all laugh. He is a regular little soldier."

Besides being allowed to write letters home, the prisoners could also have likenesses of themselves made to send home. Colonel Owen permitted a photographer to set up shop on the campgrounds. Roche offered to share some of his money so that he and Johnny could go to the photographer together. But, Johnny knew by the way his shirt hung so loosely on his shoulders and the way he had to hitch up his belt that he had lost a lot of weight. If his ma saw him that way, she would only worry about him.

Johnny said, "That's mighty nice of you, but I'll wait a while for a picture. Thank you kindly."

Johnny had a hard time finishing his letter. He finally ended with, "I can't wait to get home and see you all." That was true. What he couldn't say truthfully was that he didn't know when, or if, he would ever get to go home again.

A Petition for Johnny

IT HAD NOW BEEN NEARLY A WEEK since the Confederate soldiers had been surrendered at Fort Donelson and sent to Camp Morton. No matter how kind Colonel Owen was, most of the Southern prisoners were miserable in the North.

The weather in Indiana was cold, much colder than any of them were accustomed to. The drainage in the camp was so poor that the ground stayed wet and muddy. This meant that their shoes were damp most of the time. Many of the prisoners were ill. Some of them had health problems even before they arrived at Camp Morton. There had been an outbreak of measles at Fort Donelson. Other men had suffered from typhoid fever. The effects of exposure and hunger on the battlefield plus the suffering on the journey to Indianapolis had taken its toll. A great many of the prisoners became ill after they arrived. Hardly a day passed without a death at Camp Morton.

The men of Company C were deeply saddened when they learned that Private Joseph W. Williams died on the first day of March. He was buried in a small Indianapolis cemetery. It was a bitter blow for the Red Invincibles to know that their comrade had found his final resting place in the frozen Northern ground. One of the men wrote a letter to Williams's family back in Mississippi to let them know the sad news.

The day after Williams died, another prisoner from the 4th Mississippi Regiment died. Other men from this regiment died during the month of March also. The report of each death was a painful wound for the prisoners.

In the gloom of an Indiana winter, many of the men grew depressed. Johnny fell victim to this same malady. Despite Roche's efforts to cheer Johnny, his friend grew sadder with each passing day. There were times he refused to leave his bunk in the dark barracks. He lay staring at the walls.

After he mailed his letter home, he had gone eagerly to mail call each day. He watched as other prisoners began to receive letters and packages from home, but Johnny was disappointed when he did not hear his name.

Roche tried to help Johnny think of reasons why he didn't receive any letters from home. "Don't give up too soon," he said. "There's no way of knowing how long it takes for mail to get to Kentucky from this place. Maybe your ma just got your letter today. Think how happy it will make her to hear from you."

Johnny supposed Roche was right, but it was getting harder and harder for him to keep his hopes up. The cold, gray days didn't help lift his spirits either. When there was no response to his letter after a few days, Johnny seemed to retreat into his own world. He pulled his blanket tighter around his thin body. Sometimes he even covered his ears when it was time for mail call in the afternoon. When Roche looked at Johnny, wrapped up that way, it reminded him of the time he'd seen his dead father laid out just before he was buried. It sent a shiver along Roche's spine.

All of the Mississippi men in the barracks were worried about Johnny. He had seemed a scrawny, young lad when the Red Invincibles had first found him and made him go along with them to cut wood. The days and nights in the bitter cold on the battlefield at Fort Donelson had been a nightmare. The long trip North had been hard for everyone, an ordeal that only the hardiest person could endure. Johnny seemed to suffer a great deal more than many of them did. Perhaps it was because he was so homesick for his family. All of these things took their toll on his health. The men began to talk in whispers among themselves about the boy they fondly called "Sprout."

"He wouldn't be here if we hadn't taken him with us to Fort Donelson," Wallace said.

"It would be terrible if he . . . if he . . ." Roche, remembering his dead father, could not bring himself to finish his sentence.

"I know," Cade said. "He's pining away. What that boy needs is to be back with his family in Kentucky."

Each day, the prisoners watched Johnny as he grew weaker. He took little or no interest in anything.

"You've got to eat something, Sprout." They took turns trying to tempt him with choice bits of their own rations. When

Hamilton received another package of jam, he managed to bribe one of the guards who let him take a small jar for Johnny.

One of the men from Company E managed to carve a wooden whistle before the guards discovered his knife and took it away from him. The whittler played a jiggy little tune on the whistle and then handed it to Johnny. Johnny nodded his thanks but just lay looking at the whistle.

"I can teach you how to play 'Turkey in the Straw' with it," the man offered. But Johnny did not seem interested.

Then, Roche had an idea. He went out to see if he could locate the Kentucky man who had the dog. When he found him, he told the man about Johnny. "Maybe it would help if Frank would pay a call on him. Johnny thought Frank was a right smart dog."

Roche entered the door of the barracks and knelt by Johnny's bunk. "Look who came to pay you a visit," he said.

At a signal from his master, Frank wagged his tail and jumped up on Johnny's bed. But, Johnny only stared dully as the dog licked his face.

The men of Company C talked about what they could do to help.

"We could dig an escape tunnel."

"Not with the ground frozen almost hard."

"Maybe we could scale the walls."

"Or create a diversion while we help him sneak out of camp."

They knew, however, that Johnny did not have the strength to try any sort of shenanigans.

"Maybe you could bribe one of the guards," Cade said to Hamilton.

"Not for something like that I couldn't," Hamilton replied.

"Well, I noticed that some of the men are sending letters to the governor and writing petitions to Colonel Owen," Cade said. "Maybe we could do that and explain why Sprout is not supposed to be here."

The more the men talked about it, the more they felt that this was the best idea. They believed they could trust the colonel to give them a fair hearing. They took up a collection, and everyone who had a few coins pitched them into Hamilton's hat. He went to the sutler and purchased paper and ink. When he returned he handed the items to Cade.

"What am I going to do with this?" Cade wanted to know.

"You're going to write the petition. After all, it was your idea," Hamilton said.

Cade handed the paper to Robert Patton, a soldier in Company E who had the reputation of being a good writer. "I think you would do a better job with this sort of thing."

Patton looked at the paper. "I reckon I can write it, but you all will have to help me figure out what to say."

The men of companies C and E gathered around Patton as they labored over the words. Everyone had suggestions about what ought to be included, and they all talked at once. They had called the boy "Sprout" for so long, it took a few minutes for them to remember that his name was John W. Ables.

"Be sure to write down that he's only fourteen years of age," Roche said.

"Be sure you make clear that we forced him to come with us to cut wood," Cade added.

The suggestions came so fast that Patton could hardly get them on paper.

"Say that he's not a soldier. That's important."

"Put down that he's not supposed to be here."

"Tell that he lived with his mother, and she's a widow."

Patton repeated each sentence aloud before he wrote it. He made certain that everyone agreed with what he was going to write. They could not afford for him to make a mistake and waste the paper they had bought with their precious little bit of money. It took a long time for him to get all the words written down.

When he was finished, Patton read the petition aloud as the men listened carefully:

"We the undersigned do hereby certify that John W. Ables, (a boy 14 years old) who lives in Calloway County, Ky was, with his wagon & horses pressed into the service of the C.S.A. for the purpose of Hauling wood, for the Army, and we do further certify that the said J. W. Ables was taken to Fort Donelson by the Army of the C. S. and was present at the Surrender of said Fort. We do further certify that said Jno. W. Ables is not, and has not been enlisted in, or by his consent acting with the C. S. Army; but that he is a private citizen of Calloway County, Ky. And was at

*the time above mentioned living with his mother who is a
widow and a resident of said Co."*

When Patton had finished reading the petition aloud to
them, he looked at the men huddled around him. One by one
they nodded in agreement. No one could think of anything to
change or to add. The petition seemed to them as good as if a
lawyer had written it. When he knew that everyone approved
what he had written, Patton wrote, *Camp Morton Ind.* He then
dated the petition, *March 6th 1862.*

One by one men in Company C and Company E of the
4th Mississippi Regiment of Volunteers stepped forward and
took turns putting their names on the petition. Not every
man could write his name. A few had to have help from a
comrade. Patton's signature was followed by those of John
McCarrell, Samuel Knox Ingram, W. H. Habors, S. W. King,
E. T. Stoker, George W. Collins, and many others. It took a
long time for eighty-five of the men to sign the petition, but
finally the last two names were added. They were F. M. White
and S. White.

Cade probably spoke for all the men as he said, "When
Colonel Owen sees this, he will have to agree that Johnny
Ables should be set free and allowed to go back to his home in
Kentucky."

"When I tell Johnny about this petition, he's going to feel
a lot better," Roche said. "I know he will."

"Wait just a minute," Cade reached out and put his hand
on Roche's arm. "We'd best not say anything to Sprout until we

We the undersigned do hereby certify that John
W. Ables, (a boy 14 years old) who lives in Calloway
county Ky, was, with his wagon & horses pressed
into the service of the C. S. A. for the purpose of
Hauling wood, for the army, and we do further
certify, that the said J. W. Ables was taken to Fort
Donelson by the army of the C. S. and was
present at the Surrender of said fort. We do
further certify that said Jno. W. Ables is not, and
has not been enlisted in, or by his consent acting
with the C. S. Army; but that he is a private
citizen of Calloway county, Ky, and was at
the time above mentioned living with his mother
who is a widow and a resident of said Co.
Camp Morton Ind.
          March 6th 1862   R, Patton
Names   John McCorral
S, K, Ingram   E, T, Stoker
H, H, Nabors   W, A, Stafford
S, W, King   J, G, Holmes
J, L, Harris   R, P, Holmes
W, C, Pittman   G, W, Trainer
J, A, Pyron   W, M, Nabers
W, H, Wray   D, A, Naber
S, P, Baker   G, F, Collin
R, J, Pittman   G, E, Simmons

Petition written to Colonel Richard Owen requesting that Johnny Ables be freed from prison and
allowed to return home.

D. M. Wray
R. Gray
Jab. Geray
John Britt
B. C. Pace
W. J. Harris
J. J. Gearly
R. J. Curtis
H. L. Foreham
J. P. Ford
J. J. King
F. L. King
W. A. Curtis
A. P. Townsend
A. A. Matkin
Wm. Ro Wright
J. B. Davis
J. J. Moore
A. A. Carmical
D. F. Hodge
Thomas Hird
R. D. Sih
R. J. Moore
J. J. Spoks
C. W. McCain
J. M. William
J. F. Hendrick
C. B. Brasier

John McSwain
James Scruse
J. M. Hendrix
C. H. Music
Carter Sartain
Bevil Odle
J. M. Holmes Co. (C.)
J. H. Booth
K. M. Williams
H. L. Wallace
Ith. Alexander
J. R. Young
J. J. Slaton
B. F. Thompson
W. J. Dawson
J. L. Grimshaw
Henry Wilfster
W. B. Smith
J. W. Goss
B. F. Huffman
W. L. Johnson
J. W. Smith
J. M. Spratt
W. R. Cade
W. F. Willis
M. L. Johnson
W. D. Thompson
J. H. Harrison

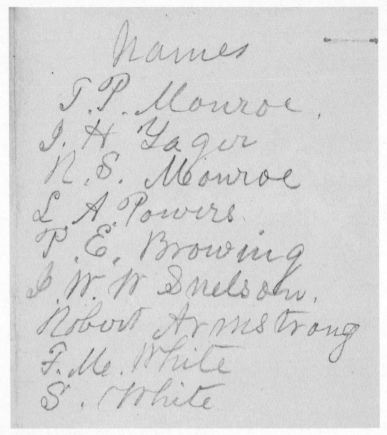

Last of the signatures on the petition for John W. Ables.

have some good news to tell him. If he gets his hopes up and nothing comes of it, it might set him back."

Roche nodded. He thought about Johnny's disappointment when he hadn't received any letters from home. He understood what Cade was saying. Even though he was certain that

Colonel Owen would help, what if he didn't? Roche didn't even want to think that it could be otherwise.

"Can I take the petition to Colonel Owen?" Roche wanted to know, but the men decided that since the petition was Cade's idea he should do it. Cade was older and might have more authority.

The men watched as Cade walked across the grounds to Colonel Owen's office. Cade talked with the Union officer who stood guard at the office door. Roche's heart sank as he saw the guard shaking his head. Cade continued to talk. He held the petition out to the guard. There was a big sigh of relief from all the men when the guard finally took the paper and then nodded.

Cade returned to the cluster of waiting prisoners and explained what had happened. "The guard said Colonel Owen is very busy right now. He gave orders that he wasn't to be disturbed by anyone. The guard said that he would try his best to deliver the petition as soon as possible."

"Do you think he will—I mean, do you think the guard will deliver it?" Patton asked.

Cade said, "We have to trust the guard to keep his word. That's all we can do."

The prisoners waited as patiently as they could, but it wasn't easy. As they waited, they watched Sprout, who seemed to grow worse each day. Several days went by, but the Mississippians heard nothing. Finally, Roche could stand it no longer. He walked over to the colonel's office to talk to the guard.

"Did you deliver that petition to the colonel like you said you would?"

The guard nodded. Roche stood looking at the guard for a few moments. He didn't know what else to say. He didn't want to anger the man. If he got on the guard's wrong side, it might make matters worse for Johnny.

Roche went back to his barracks and sat on a log outside the doorway. He stared at Colonel Owen's closed office door. It was as though by thinking as hard as he could, Roche would be able to make the thing he wished for come to pass.

More days went by and all the prisoners had unspoken questions on their minds. Why didn't Colonel Owen respond? Should they write another petition? They spent many hours arguing among themselves about what they should do. In the end, all they could do was to hope that time would not run out for Johnny.

What the prisoners did not know was that Colonel Richard Owen faced an almost impossible task. He had more work than one man was able to do by himself. He worked all day, every day, and often late into the night. Johnny's fate was now in his hands.

11

Will Johnny Go Free?

COLONEL OWEN AWAKENED when he heard a knock on the door. A new day had begun, but he could hardly remember exactly which day it was. All of his days seemed to run together. He sighed and sat up reluctantly. He had spent another night sleeping in his uniform on the small cot in his office at Camp Morton. Not once since the prisoners had arrived had he been able to go to the hotel for a good night's sleep or to eat a relaxing meal in pleasant surroundings. Sometimes it seemed that he, himself, was a prisoner at the camp.

There was a second knock, this time louder.

"Enter," he called wearily.

The door opened, and his aide came in, carrying a tray of food. The colonel pulled on his boots and stood up.

"Thank you," he said to the aide. "Just put the tray on my desk."

As Colonel Owen looked at his desk, he realized there was no room for the tray there. His desk was piled high with papers.

He shrugged and said, "I guess you will just have to put the tray on the chair.

The aide did as he was told and left.

Owen sat down again on the edge of the cot and pulled the chair closer to him. He could use it as a make-shift table. He looked at the food on the tray. It was not at all appetizing to him. He thought about how breakfast time used to be at his home in New Harmony. That had been one of the best times of each day. He relished sitting at the Owen dining table and looking at the dear faces of his wife and other family members who were gathered around.

He shook his head to rid himself of these thoughts. After all, this was wartime; everyone had to make sacrifices. There were thousands of men in this prison camp eating the same kind of rations he had been served. And there were hundreds of thousands more soldiers in the field who would think this breakfast fit for a king. His own son was somewhere on a battlefield. He was ashamed at feeling sorry for himself. Owen dutifully took a couple of bites of food and then placed the tray on the floor by the door for the aide to remove later.

Again he stood up and looked at his desk. There was much work to be done. There were several reports to be written; he had to answer dozens of letters; and he had to look over the accounts of money spent to operate the camp and make sure they were all correct. Numerous items of business had to be taken care of in order to manage a prison the size of Camp Morton.

"Where should I start?" he asked himself aloud. He was a bit embarrassed when he realized that he was beginning to talk to himself more often these days, but it helped him unravel the tangle of thoughts in his head if he could put them into spoken words.

He called his aide back into the room. "I'm going to make a list of the items that need attention. Or rather, you can make the list while I talk," Owen told the aide.

Colonel Owen paced back and forth across the small room. The aide waited patiently, with paper at the ready.

"Food. That is the first order of business. Put that at the top of the list." Owen was aware that people who are not well fed will be dissatisfied. Such dissatisfaction could lead to serious trouble. He had heard many complaints about the food at the prison, and he tried to consider them carefully. Owen knew very well that all soldiers, no matter what side they are on, gripe about army food. However, he felt some of the complaints were justified.

He had heard a lot of grumbling about the bread. It occurred to him that this problem might be solved if the camp had its own bakery. He must figure out a way to get this done. The first step would be to convince his superior officers that baking bread right there on the grounds would save money as well as provide a measure of contentment. Reliable prisoners could do the baking; it would give them something useful to do, and the bread would satisfy their particular tastes.

"Yes," the colonel said to the aide, "put a bakery on the list."

Colonel Owen also knew that more barracks were needed. There were large groups of Southern soldiers being kept temporarily in other Indiana towns. They should all be brought to Camp Morton as soon as possible.

Poor drainage on the campground was also a problem. Every time there was a hard rain, the creek that ran through the campground overflowed. He would have to order lumber and build plank walkways. No doubt, some of the guards and the prisoners were ill because they were ankle-deep in mud whenever they walked on the prison grounds.

A bakery. More barracks. Walkways. All of these projects would cost money. Owen knew that he had to find funding for all of them. And some problems could not be solved by money. A group of Kentuckians had created another kind of difficulty. They had made the trip to Indianapolis, hoping to see family members and friends who were in Camp Morton. Owen had

Confederate prisoners at Camp Morton Prison nicknamed this stream, running through the middle of the camp, "The Potomac."

firm orders that such visits were not to be permitted. He had published this information in the *Louisville Journal*; however, many had come in spite of that. They waited outside the gates daily. He knew he must take a firm stand against their pleadings. That would be difficult because he understood and felt sorry for them.

Another problem he had to deal with were the charitable groups, such as the Ladies Patriotic Society and the Sanitary Commission, which had contacted him. They offered to provide blankets, money, clothing, and other necessary items for the prisoners. All of these things would have to be distributed fairly.

"The next item for the list is straw," Owen said to the aide. "We need more straw for the beds."

The aide looked up and said, "Straw is a problem, sir. The prisoners will not stop smoking in the barracks. There have been several fires."

Owen was well aware of that. He nodded and sighed. Why was it that the solution of one problem always seemed to lead to another? Straw would make the beds more comfortable and warmer, but it was also a safety hazard.

"We need outdoor clothing lines," Colonel Owen added. "The prisoners need to wash their clothing and have a place to hang it out to dry." He also believed that they needed to air their blankets regularly and that the men had to keep clean or even more of them would become ill. The number of prisoners that had sickened was growing daily. "Mark that item as urgent, Sergeant."

This photograph of Confederate prisoners outside the wooden barracks at Camp Morton Prison, which was taken in the late summer of 1864, shows that prisoners were allowed to hang their wet laundry outside their barracks as Colonel Owen had planned.

"The sutlers are a problem, too," Colonel Owen said to the aide as he picked up a large pile of papers from his desk. "Every one of these is a request from a merchant. They all want permission to set up shop inside the gates and sell things to the prisoners. There is just not enough space for all of them."

"Some of the sutlers cheat the prisoners by overcharging them, sir," the aide replied.

The colonel shook his head in disgust and said, "I want you to ask the Confederate sergeants which of the sutlers treat the prisoners unfairly. Perhaps if we weed out a few of the bad ones that will make more room for the good ones."

The list the aide was making grew longer as the colonel paced and talked. He had to decide what to do about a letter he had received from a man who complained that some storekeepers were smuggling knives into the camp. Owen knew from his own observations that most of the knives were small ones and were used by prisoners who wanted to pass the time by whittling or carving. He sat down at his desk, rubbing his temples, as he wondered what to do about this. He didn't think there was any harm in a man whittling, but if one unfortunate incident occurred, it could cause a great deal of trouble. Finally, he shook his head unhappily and said, "Make a note that all knives must be taken away from the prisoners."

There was one stack of papers on the far corner of Owen's desk that seemed to grow larger each passing day. Despite the fact that he promised himself to deal with as many of them as he could daily, the pile never got smaller. These papers were petitions—dozens of them. They came from the prisoners and their families. The men from companies C and E of the 4th Mississippi were not the only ones who had a matter of importance that they wanted to put before the colonel.

The clock over the door struck twelve times. The colonel had worked all morning without a break. He stretched and said to his aide, "You'd better go and eat your lunch now."

"Thank you, sir," the aide replied. "I'll bring your lunch tray around before I eat."

"No need to bother. I'm much too busy to eat." Colonel Owen picked up the petition on the top of the pile to see what these folks wanted. Petitions were never easy to deal with. He knew how important each and every problem was to the person who faced it. He wished it were possible for him to grant each request, but that simply was not in his power. He was able to take care of many things such as better food and more blankets. However, many of the requests he received asked for the impossible.

The first three petitions were from prisoners who promised that if they were allowed to leave Camp Morton, they would sign an oath of allegiance to the Union and not fight against the United States ever again. They stated that they wanted to stay in Indianapolis, get a job, and make their homes in the North. If he said, "yes," to every petition like these, it would mean letting half the prisoners in Camp Morton walk out of the gates. He shook his head as he put these petitions in the stack to be denied.

He reached for the next petition, and what he read astonished him. This was somewhat different from other petitions that were usually placed on his desk. This petition was signed by dozens of prisoners, their names filling two-and-a-half pages. He turned back to the beginning of the petition and read it all the way through. Then he read it a second time just to make certain that he understood it correctly.

Owen stood and pushed back his chair. He called to the Union guard standing outside his office door. He started to ask the soldier to go to the barracks where the 4th Mississippi was located, but then he changed his mind. He would do this errand himself. As he opened his office door, his aide started to enter with his noon meal. Colonel Owen put out his hand and said, "I haven't got time for food now. I must see if a terrible injustice has been done."

Owen walked quickly across the campgrounds, pausing only briefly to speak with several prisoners who called out to him. When he reached one of the barracks where the Mississippi men were housed, he saw a prisoner sitting on a log outside the door. He held the petition out to him and asked, "Do you know anything about this?"

Roche was the prisoner on the log. He jumped up and said, "Yes, sir. That is our petition."

"Where would I find the boy named John W. Ables?"

Roche led the colonel inside the dark, foul-smelling room. He walked between the rows of bunks until he found Johnny curled up tightly in a blanket with his face to the wall. Owen squinted trying to see the boy in the cave-like gloom.

"Do you have a candle?" the colonel asked. Quickly Roche produced one and lit it from the fire in the woodstove. He held the candle up high to light the room.

Colonel Owen sat down on the edge of Johnny's bunk. Gently he put his hand on the boy's shoulder. "John . . . are you John Ables?" the colonel asked.

At first Johnny didn't move. Then he slowly opened his eyes. He saw the candle light flickering against the barracks wall. Johnny had been dreaming about home. He thought the gentle touch was his mother. He thought she had put a candle in the window to guide him home.

The colonel called to him again. Johnny rolled over. It took a minute for the dream to fade. When he was fully awake and saw who it was sitting beside him, he sat up quickly and tried to rise.

"Stay where you are," the colonel said.

Johnny's heart pounded when he saw Colonel Owen. He didn't understand what was happening. Perhaps he was dreaming again. Why was the camp commandant here? Johnny wondered if he had broken some campground rule and was in trouble. Then he saw that the expression on Colonel Owen's face was friendly.

Word had spread quickly about Owen's visit. As many as possible of the Mississippi men had crowded into the barracks and shoved near Johnny's bunk. Everyone waited quietly until the colonel spoke.

"Well now, son, I understand that you are not supposed to be here in prison." In response, Johnny poured out his entire story. He told about how he had left home to cut wood and was taken to Fort Donelson by the 4th Mississippi.

"Were you there during the battle?" Colonel Owen asked.

Johnny nodded. He hoped he wouldn't have to tell about what he had seen or heard. He didn't want to think about those awful days of battle or the trip north.

Colonel Owen was silent for a long time. He looked at this frail young boy. He thought about his own children. He knew how he would feel if one of them was in Johnny's position. There was complete silence inside the barracks for several minutes.

"I cannot make any promises to you," Colonel Owen said softly. "But I can tell you that I will do everything in my power to help you."

Johnny could barely speak, but he managed to say, "Thank you, sir." These words seemed to echo through the barracks as each of the men said, "Thank you. Thank you. Thank you, sir."

As Colonel Owen left the barracks, the prisoners respect-fully moved back and made a passageway for him. After he had gone, no one said anything for a while, but each prisoner was wondering the same thing: Was Johnny going to go free?

12

Johnny Leaves Prison

WHEN COLONEL OWEN RETURNED to his office, he put aside all of his other work. The matter of John W. Ables was uppermost in his mind at that moment. He looked at his calendar. It was now the eighteenth day of March. This petition had been written on March sixth, so almost two weeks had gone by. Something had to be done about Ables, and it had to be done right away. Quickly, he penned a letter to Governor Oliver P. Morton.

> *Sir:*
> *A peculiar case exists among the Prisoners at Camp Morton, under my charge, the particulars of which it appears my duty to present to your notice.*
> *A boy, fourteen years of age, named John Abels, was, according to the testimony of the entire company with which I found him, pressed into the service of the Southern Army with his team, while hauling wood, near Fort Henry.*

His mother is a widow with two small children and John himself seems small & weakly for his age. He is at present with Co. "C" 4th Mississippi regiment.

"Very respectfully,
Yr obt. Servt
Richard Owen Col. 60th Indiana
Comdg Camp

His Excellency   Camp Morton
Governor O.P. Morton   18 March 1862
                        Sir
                                A peculiar case exists among
the Prisoners in Camp Morton, under my charge, the par-
ticulars of which it appears my duty to present to your
notice.
A boy, fourteen years of age, named John Abels, was,
according to the testimony of the entire company with
which I found him, pressed into the service of the
southern army with his team, while hauling wood,
near Fort Henry.
His mother is a widow with two small children
& John himself seems small & weakly for his age.
He is at present with "C" 4th Mississippi Regiment.
                        my resptfly
                        Yr obt Servt
                        Richard Owen Col 60th Ind.
                        Comdg Camp.

Colonel Owen called his aide and instructed him to see that the letter was delivered immediately to Governor Morton.

Surprisingly, the letter quickly made its way from the governor to the adjutant general of the State of Indiana, Lazarus Noble. General Noble acted upon the matter right away. The day after Colonel Owen had spoken to Johnny, a decision was made. Owen received the answer on March 19, 1862, almost a

Letter from Colonel Richard Owen to Governor Oliver Morton explaining Johnny Ables's situation, dated March 18, 1862, with an added testament as to the accuracy of Owen's account. Note the signatures of two of the soldiers from Company C, 4th Mississippi Regiment, who are familiar characters in this story: W. R. (William) Cade and J. E. (Johnny) Roche.

month after Johnny and the other prisoners had arrived at the prison camp in Indianapolis. Johnny was no longer a prisoner. He was to be set at liberty.

Colonel Owen knew that just because Johnny was free to leave the prison, his problems would not end. He sent for Johnny to come to his office. There were some important matters they had to discuss.

Johnny sat on a chair near the colonel's desk, shivering not only with cold but with excitement. He could hardly believe the good news that he could leave the prison camp. He was free to go home to his mother and little sisters.

"Going back to Kentucky will not be easy for you," Colonel Owen explained. "You are several hundreds of miles from your home. You will have to travel by yourself and find your own way." The colonel paused and looked at Johnny. It took a while for the meaning of his words to sink in.

Johnny thought of all that had happened since he left Calloway County in early February. In his mind, he thought of that day he set out with his horses and the wagon to cut wood. He recalled how he met up with the Mississippi soldiers who took him to Fort Donelson. He did not want to remember the battle, nor did he like to think about the terrible boat trip on the river or the train trip to Indianapolis. He wanted to put all of that behind him. Instead he thought about those words, "You can go home now."

Colonel Owen said, "I will do everything I can to help you make the journey back to Kentucky." The colonel wrote something on a piece of paper and handed it to Johnny. "This is a pass for you to use as you travel. The adjutant general himself, Lazarus Noble, recommended that I provide you with a pass to help you on your journey home."

Johnny stared at the words the colonel had written. He didn't understand what they meant. The colonel explained, "This pass is in your name and signed by me. If anyone stops you, it will explain why you have been in the North and why you are traveling to the South. It also asks that railroad and steamboat agents allow you to ride free. Do you understand?"

Johnny nodded.

"Now, mind you," Colonel Owen warned, "Just because I requested that you be allowed to ride free, it does not mean the agents have to let you do so. I am counting on their good will." The colonel continued, "I will have my aide make a list of places where you should go to board the trains and boats to help you find your way."

By now Johnny's head was spinning. There were going to be so many things for him to remember. The colonel understood that this was a lot for a boy Johnny's age to take on by himself, especially for a boy as sickly as Johnny seemed to be.

"Are you certain you are up to this? You don't have to go if you think you cannot make it by yourself."

Johnny paused only for a moment. He knew that he wanted to leave this place and to be with his family again. "I want to go home," he said firmly.

"You may leave tomorrow if you wish."

Johnny took a very deep breath. It was almost too much for him to take in. He could not speak, so he merely nodded.

"Very well," Colonel Owen said. "Go back to your barracks and collect all your possessions."

Johnny stood. He felt quite shaken with the excitement of it all, but he did manage to say, "Thank you, sir. Thank you very much."

It did not take long for Johnny to gather his belongings. He didn't really have anything except the blanket he had been given and the wooden whistle that one of the prisoners had carved for him. But, he did have some unfinished business. He wanted to thank the men of Company C and Company E for writing the petition. If it hadn't been for them, he would have stayed in Camp Morton with the rest of the prisoners.

Johnny also wanted to say "goodbye" to Roche and the others, but it would not be easy. No matter how happy Johnny was to be leaving Camp Morton, he knew that his friends would not be going home. They would still be prisoners, and he was sad for them.

When it came right down to it, neither Johnny nor Roche could utter the word "goodbye." Several times Johnny opened his mouth. There was too much to say, and yet he could not speak. Johnny remembered all that he and Roche had shared together during the past several weeks. They just stood and looked at each other and finally they shook hands awkwardly. Johnny knew that Roche understood what Johnny wished he could tell him.

That evening a guard came to the barracks with a package for Johnny, wrapped in brown paper and tied with a string. The guard said it was from Colonel Owen. Johnny opened it and found a pair of neat brown trousers, a jacket, and a tweed cap. There were also socks, underclothing, and a shirt. The thing that caught Johnny's attention, however, was a pair of shoes. The shoes were brown leather and appeared to be almost new. Johnny had never owned such fine shoes in all of his life. He put them on immediately. They were just a bit large, but he didn't mind; he would grow into them.

Johnny could hardly sleep that night. When he got up, it was barely light. Quietly, so as not to disturb the other prisoners, he dressed in his new clothes. He did not put on his new shoes, however. Instead, he pulled on his worn and misshapen old ones. He did not want to spoil the new ones by walking across the muddy campground. He could put them on later. Fully dressed, he sat on the edge of his bunk until it was light and the other prisoners were awake and ready to move about. Then Johnny stood and left the barracks.

Although it was very early, many of the prisoners turned out to wish him well and to wave at him as he left. The Kentucky soldier was there with Frank at his side. Johnny bent down to scratch the dog's ears. He buried his face in the dog's neck to keep the others from seeing the tears that had come into his eyes at the thought of leaving these people who were now his friends.

Slowly Johnny walked to Colonel Owen's office, and the guard opened the door to admit him. Colonel Owen was hard at work at his desk. He stood up, came over to Johnny, and looked carefully at him, inspecting him from head to toe.

"You look fine," the colonel said. "Just like a young squire."

Once again, Johnny had no words, but he did manage a smile.

Colonel Owen picked up a small package and handed it to Johnny. "Here is something for you to eat when you travel. You need to keep up your strength." The colonel's words reminded Johnny of what his ma had said that day so long ago when he had left home to cut wood.

Johnny listened as Colonel Owen ordered his own buggy to be brought to the gate. He said, "My aide will take you to the railroad station. He will see to it that you get safely on the train heading to Terre Haute."

As Johnny started to climb into the buggy, the colonel added, "Take good care of your pass. Don't show it to anyone except an official of the railroad or the steamboat." Then Colonel Owen slipped some coins into Johnny's pocket.

The colonel's aide snapped the lines smartly over the horses' backs, and Johnny felt them move forward. The buggy rolled briskly through the gate, leaving the tall wooden enclosure behind. Johnny looked back and saw the words emblazoned across the entrance: "MILITARY PRISON: CAMP MORTON." He watched until he could no longer read those hateful words. He kept looking back until he could no longer see the Union guards, with their rifles, walking the platform surrounding the wall that had kept him captive.

When he finally turned around, Johnny was aware that even though he had left the prison behind, it would be a part of him forever. So would the many horrible events of the past six weeks. He had wounds buried deep inside where nobody could see. These were the kinds of wounds that scarred the memory. He sensed that his experience had changed him in ways he did not yet fully understand.

When the buggy reached the railroad station, Johnny stepped out onto the crowded platform. People with boxes and bundles moved hurriedly toward the train. Handing Johnny a list of places to board trains and boats, the aide said, "This is the train that will take you to Terre Haute. You'll have to change trains there and get one headed south for Evansville. That's where you ought to be able to get a steamboat going downriver. Have you got the pass that the colonel made for you?"

Johnny put his hand into his jacket pocket and felt the piece of paper and the coins Colonel Owen had given him. He patted his pocket and said, "Yes, I have everything."

"There's the conductor. Show him your pass," the aide said. "I'll wait here until you're onboard, and the train leaves the station."

Johnny looked at the waiting locomotive as it chuffed out dark smoke. The whistle shrieked. He thought the train looked like a crouching black monster waiting to swallow him. Colonel Owen had warned Johnny that trying to get home would not be easy. He was moving out into the unknown again, just as he had that day the Mississippi soldiers had forced him to go with them. This time he would be all alone, though. Who could say what might happen to him along the way?

Johnny hesitated. His heart was thumping wildly. He thought about asking the aide to take him back to Camp

Morton. At least it was a familiar place to him. He had friends there who cared about him. Just then, the whistle sounded once more. He paused and turned toward the carriage. The aide nodded his head in the direction of the conductor and gave Johnny an encouraging smile and a snappy salute. "Good luck," he called out.

"What is wrong with me?" Johnny wondered. He was free at last; why would he think, even for one moment, about going back to that prison camp? He was free to go home and be with his family—something he had thought about and dreamed about every day and night since he was captured. He was free to make his own choices: to go or to stay. It was up to him now.

Johnny looked once more at the buggy where the aide waited. He raised his hand and waved. Then, he turned and walked quickly toward the conductor and held out the pass that Colonel Owen had written for him. The busy conductor had his hands full of papers, tickets, and schedules, but he managed to take Johnny's pass. "What's this, now?" he asked Johnny, peering over the top of his glasses at him.

"It's a pass, sir."

"Oh, a pass, is it? Well, lad, this train is mighty full of people. All of the trains are jam-packed these days. Lots of soldier boys are riding free. Hardly room enough for paying passengers, and there are plenty of them wanting to go places. But, here you are, and you want me to let you ride free?"

Johnny could hardly breathe. He was sure the conductor would turn him away. At last, though, the conductor said, "It's a good thing you're not very big. We can probably squeeze you in somewhere." As soon as he heard that, Johnny hurried to join the other people waiting to board the train.

"You'll have to stand," the conductor called out to him. "Every seat is taken."

"Thank you, sir," Johnny called back, as he clambered aboard. "I'll manage just fine."

He knew that, indeed, he would manage. It might not be easy, but he was heading home at last. Johnny glanced down at his garments. He half expected to see himself still wearing the mud-caked clothing he had worn when he was first marched into Camp Morton Prison. He had to reassure himself that he was dressed in a decent jacket and pants, and he had on new shoes. He even had a few coins jingling in his pocket. Better yet, he felt confident. No matter what happened next, Johnny Ables was on his way home.

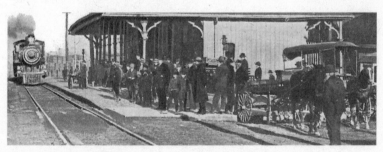

This photograph shows a railroad scene very much like the one Johnny must have encountered as he left the custody of Camp Morton Prison and began his journey home.

Afterword

What Happened to Johnny Ables?
If this were a made-up story, the author could easily decide Johnny's fate and satisfy the natural desire for a neatly drawn conclusion. However, this story actually happened to a real boy, and sometimes real-life endings to stories cannot be known.

Throughout history, thousands of persons have been reported missing as a result of wars being fought. Their families waited at home and wondered what happened to them. In the case of Johnny Ables, the story of what his family members back in Calloway County, Kentucky, were doing after his disappearance must be left to the imagination. No doubt they were puzzled as to why Johnny did not return home after he set off that February morning to cut wood. His mother may have feared that he had injured himself in an accident. Had a tree fallen on him? Had he wounded himself with the ax? Relatives and friends probably went out to search for him, mystified when they did not find even the slightest trace of Johnny, the wagon, or the horses.

In a similar manner, only imagination can describe Johnny's trip home. As he started out on this lonely adventure trying to make his way back to Kentucky, did memories of the terrible journey north come back to haunt him? Did he remember the cold and the hunger of that trip? Was he lucky enough to meet up with kind persons who helped him make it home safely? Did friendly conductors on the railroad and ticket agents for the steamboats permit him to ride free? Or, did he find unsympathetic officials who refused him passage?

Perhaps Johnny's journey was made difficult or even dangerous by people who sought to take advantage of a young boy traveling by himself. Perhaps "thugs" tried to rob him of his money, food, nice clothing, or traveling pass. During Civil War times, trains were often derailed or involved in deadly collisions. Several steamboats exploded, and many people were killed as a result. Was Johnny able to survive all the dangers that a traveler might have encountered during wartime?

There is no way to know how long it took Johnny to get home, or, if he was lucky enough to arrive home safely, what he found when he got there. Was he welcomed with relief and joy at his return? Or, had his family given up ever seeing him again? Perhaps his mother had taken his little sisters and moved to Tennessee to live with his aunt. Did Johnny have to continue his long journey to search for his family?

Johnny's wartime ordeal probably would not have ended with his return home. He might have had nightmares about some of the horrors he had witnessed. Johnny was described as being small for his age and "weakly." His experiences during the Battle of Fort Donelson and the horrible trip north where he endured cold and hunger surely took their toll. It is true that Colonel Richard Owen was a decent man, who tried to make Camp Morton a humane prison facility. However, being penned up in a prison camp surrounded by armed guards was a harsh experience that would have been burned into Johnny's memory.

For now, there is only our imagination. What happened to Johnny? Did he settle down to live happily ever after? Other than one clue, this question cannot be answered. The 1870 census record for the state of Tennessee provides an interesting bit of information: In Fayette County, there is a listing for a young man named John Abels. This John was about the same age that Johnny would have been in the year 1870. Although the name recorded on the census is shown as "Abels" rather than "Ables," such variations in spellings of names were not unusual in the past. It should be recalled that the guard at Camp Morton spelled Johnny's named differently than Johnny did on the roster that first day at the prison in Indianapolis. His name was spelled "Ables" on the petition the Confederate soldiers wrote, but Colonel Owen spelled it "Abels" on the letter he wrote to Governor Morton. Could the John Abels on the 1870 census be the Johnny Ables of our story?

We do not know the ending to Johnny's story. Many questions remain with no definite answers. What do *you* think happened to Johnny Ables?

What Happened to . . . ?

Although we do not know exactly what happened to Johnny Ables after he left Camp Morton, we do know some things that will interest the readers of Johnny's story.

The 4th Mississippi Infantry Regiment: Five or six months after Johnny Ables was allowed to leave Camp Morton, the Mississippi soldiers were exchanged for Union prisoners. The soldiers were allowed to return home; however, most of them went back into the Confederate army to fight for the South.

Sumner Archibald Cunningham: Cunningham, the young Confederate soldier who urged his comrades to march with their heads high, did make a mark for himself. When the prisoners at Camp Morton were exchanged in late August of 1862, the 41st Tennessee went back into battle again, and Cunningham went with them. After the war, he returned to Tennessee where he wrote a book about his wartime experiences. He also started a magazine called *Confederate Veteran.* For many years, it was a popular publication read by Southern soldiers and their families. Cunningham led a successful campaign to raise money for a statue in honor of Colonel Richard Owen. Many of the Camp Morton prisoners contributed money to this project. This statue was dedicated in 1913 in Indianapolis and can be seen today at the Indiana Statehouse (see "Colonel Richard Owen" below). There is a copy of the statue at Purdue University.

Sumner Archibald Cunningham in later life.

Frank: The dog that brought so much pleasure to the prisoners went with his master when the soldiers were exchanged. He was soon back in battle again, where he was wounded. Unfortunately, Frank went missing in action during the summer of 1864.

Greenlawn Cemetery: Confederate prisoners who died at Camp Morton, including Mississippi private Joseph W. Williams, were first buried in a small burial ground called Greenlawn Cemetery, near the prison.* Later, the bodies of these soldiers were removed to Crown Hill Cemetery in Indianapolis. Visitors to Crown Hill may see the final resting places and brass plaques listing all the names of the Confederate prisoners who died at Camp Morton.

Camp Morton: The grounds remained a prison camp after Johnny left. However, after Colonel Richard Owen was no longer commandant, it was a very different place than it had been under his leadership. There were many complaints and scandals about the way prisoners were treated under the new camp commandant.

Colonel Richard Owen: Colonel Owen was transferred back to active duty in the Union army. He was taken prisoner at Mumfordville, Kentucky. When General Simon B. Buckner, the Confederate commander on that battlefield, heard that Owen had been captured, he rode immediately to see him. "Colonel Owen," he said, "In consideration of your kindness

This monument at Crown Hill Cemetery in Indianapolis, Indiana, marks the graves of the Confederate prisoners who died at Camp Morton.

In 1916 teachers and students of Indianapolis School #45 placed a boulder at the corner of Alabama and Nineteenth streets to mark the site of Camp Morton. The Indiana Historical Bureau installed a marker at the same location in 1962. Both historical markers were later moved to Herron–Morton Place Historical Park near the former site of Camp Morton in Indianapolis.

to prisoners at Camp Morton, you are free to go at will." When the war was over, Owen became a professor of natural history at Indiana University. During part of that time he served as president of the university. He was also appointed president of Purdue University, but never served in that capacity.

*On a plaque at Crown Hill Cemetery, Williams's name is listed incorrectly with the *Missouri* Confederate soldiers rather than with the Mississippi Confederate soldiers.

The Sons of Union Veterans, Benjamin Harrison Camp 356, placed four markers to show where the four corners of the Camp Morton property had been. One of the markers is shown here.

This memorial statue of Richard Owen sits in the Indiana State Capitol in Indianapolis, Indiana.

Glossary

Here are some words and terms that you may not know that you will find in the story of Johnny Ables. If there are other words in this story that you do not know, use your dictionary to learn what they mean.

Aide: A military officer who acts as an assistant to a superior officer.

Artillery: A branch of the army armed with heavy weapons.

Assemble: To bring together in a particular place for a purpose; to gather.

Banshee: This is a word from Irish folklore. It means a spirit, whose terrible wailing fortells a death.

Battery (batteries): Two or more pieces of artillery.

Bee tree: A tree where bees have chosen to make their hive and produce honey.

"Boys": Although many soldiers in the armies of the Civil War on both sides were young, a large number of them were older men. In spite of the age differences among them, the soldiers were commonly referred to as "boys."

Breastworks: A protected place, about chest high, built by soldiers on a battlefield.

Butternut: Many Confederate soldiers wore homemade uniforms dyed with bark from a butternut tree or walnut shells. This made the uniforms brownish in color.

Calico: A printed fabric with a pattern of figures or small flowers, used to make clothing.

Cannonading: Firing of cannons.

Certify: To promise that something is true.

Charity: Giving freely, not expecting anything in return.

Commandant: The commanding officer or the officer in charge.

Compassionate: Kind and caring about other persons.

Company: A group of soldiers within a regiment. In the Civil War a company usually consisted of about one hundred soldiers.

Comrade: A close companion, usually a member of a group such as an army buddy.

Confederate army: These were the soldiers who fought for the South. They were sometimes known as Rebels or Rebs, even Johnny Reb. Some Southern soldiers did not like to be called by the name Rebel or Reb. Some, however, thought it a badge of honor.

Corn pone (or pone): Baked or fried bread made of corn meal.

Downriver: In the direction of the water current.

Face-off: Two groups in opposition to each other.

Festive: Joyful, gay; relating to a feast or festival.

Fortification: Works built to defend a place or position (rifle pits, dugouts, trenches).

Ford: A shallow place where it is possible to cross a stream.

Frail: Physically weak, slight.

Funning: Joking, teasing, kidding.

Garrison: The troops stationed at a military post.

Gauntlet: A form of punishment in which a person or persons has to run between lines of people who hit at them with sticks. "To run the gauntlet" has become a term to describe a difficult experience.

Grub: Food.

Haversack: A pouch, usually made of canvas, carried by soldiers, holding food.

Homespun: Fabric made at home.

Hoosier: A term for persons from the state of Indiana. In the state's early days, it was not a compliment and was used to indicate a person who was rough and had no manners.

Innards: The internal organs or parts of a human or animal.

Invincible: Unbeatable.

Knapsack: A bag strapped on the back used for carrying supplies.

Latrine: Usually a pit toilet used by a great many persons, often dug in a camp setting. These were simple and did not flush.

Malady: A disease or sickness.

Menacing: Threatening, dangerous.

Minié balls: A rifle bullet with a cone-shaped head, which could be loaded quickly by dropping them down the rifle barrel. These bullets were first used in the Civil War and were named after Claude Etienne Minié, a French army officer who invented them.

Mouth organ: A musical instrument, a harmonica, played by blowing into it.

Musket: A gun with a smooth bore inside the barrel. It is not as effective as a rifle barrel, which has spiral grooves to give accuracy and distance to the bullet.

Muzzy: Confused or muddled, dazed, cannot think straight.

Oath of allegiance: A solemn promise of loyalty.

Palisade: A line of cliffs or a fence of stakes.

Parole: A pass or permission to return home.

Petition: A written request signed by one or more persons and presented to someone in authority in order to bring about a desired action.

Plagued: Afflicted by worry or distress.

Pokeweed: A rough herb with white flowers and dark purple berries.

Pone: See "cornpone" above.

Providence: The care or guidance of God or a supernatural power.

Pub: A place where alcoholic drinks are served, also known as a tavern, saloon, or bar.

Puny: Small or slight in size; weak.

Ragtag: Poorly dressed, wearing shabby clothing; messy, not neat or tidy.

Ramrod: A stick or bar used for ramming home the powder charge in a muzzle-loading weapon.

Rations: A fixed amount of something, usually food.

Ravening: To feed or devour greedily; to prowl, looking for food.

Recruiting officer: A soldier whose job is to secure the services of people for the military.

Regiment: A large army unit made up of several companies. It may consist of as many as one thousand men.

Rumor: A story that has no facts to support it. It may or may not be true.

Scrawny: Very thin and slight; puny.

Secesh: This is a nickname that some Northerners called people from the Confederate states because they had seceded (withdrawn) from the United States. The word "seceders" was shortened to "secesh."

Speechifying: An old-fashioned term for making a speech.

Snippet: A small bit.

Squire: A person of importance. The term has changed over the years. It was originally applied to a chief landowner or a person hoping to become a knight. Later it was applied to someone engaged in the practice of law.

Sutler: A storekeeper who followed an army and sold supplies to soldiers.

Terrain: The land or the earth and the way it is formed.

Tethered: An animal fastened by a rope so that it can only move within a set range.

Trace: A trail or pathway.

Trench: A ditch dug by soldiers used to protect them from enemy fire.

Union army: These were the soldiers who fought for the North. They were also known as the Federal troops and sometimes as Yankees or Yanks.

Vittles: Another word for food. It comes from an old word, victuals.

Acknowledgments

There are many individuals behind the scenes who help to make any book the finished product that the reader sees. I would like to thank some of these persons. Vicki Casteel of the Indiana State Archives has long been interested in Johnny Ables and has helped me locate information about his imprisonment at Camp Morton. Kathy Waclaw, librarian at Covington Elementary School, graciously shared her knowledge of children's literature. Judy Booe, who taught at Covington Elementary School, and her group of fifth graders read an early version of the book and gave me their suggestions. Myrna Hise, of the Covington Public Library, has assisted me on numerous occasions in obtaining research material. Professionals and volunteer workers at libraries and historical associations in Kentucky, Tennessee, and Mississippi helped me in my quest for information about these events. Amanda Jones, an intern at the Indiana Historical Society (IHS) Press, worked diligently to check all the documentation of the facts behind this story. Teresa Baer and Judith

McMullen, editors at the IHS Press, worked hard and made me work even harder, as we tried to make this book the best it could be. These editors and IHS Press editor Kathleen M. Breen helped to develop the book's storyline.

Last, but never least, I thank my husband, Dan. He is always with me every step of the way, helping whenever and however he can. He willingly drives me to anyplace the research trail leads me. He spends long, tedious, and uncomplaining hours reading documents to find the facts. He is my chief cheerleader. He picks me up, dusts me off, and gets me going again when I stumble and stub my literary toe.

Picture Credits

Chapter 1, pages 1–8
This photograph shows how Johnny Ables's wagon and team of horses may have looked as Johnny set out to gather wood for his family. (W. H. Bass Photo Co. Collection, P 0130, Indiana Historical Society).

Chapter 2, pages 9–18
Bombardment of Fort Henry, Tennessee, February 6, 1862 (*Frank Leslie's Illustrated History of the Civil War* [New York: Mrs. Frank Leslie, 1895], 152).

Effect of gunboat shells on Confederate soldiers in the woods (*Frank Leslie's Illustrated History of the Civil War* [New York: Mrs. Frank Leslie, 1895], 103).

Chapter 3, pages 19–27
"The water batteries at Fort Donelson overlooked the Cumberland River. The guns were protected by thick breastworks,

the tops of which were covered with coffee sacks filled with sand." (Sketch by H. Lovie, *Frank Leslie's Illustrated Newspaper*, March 15, 1862; repr. in Benjamin Cooling, *Forts Henry and Donelson: The Key to the Confederate Heartland* [Knoxville, TN: University of Tennessee Press, 1987], 150. Used with permission from the University of Tennessee Press).

A reproduction of one of the log huts used by the Confederate army while stationed at Fort Donelson in Tennessee (Photo taken by Daniel M. Immel at Fort Donelson State Park, Tennessee).

These fortifications inside Confederate lines are similar to the rifle pits that the Red Invincibles dug to protect themselves during the Battle of Fort Donelson. (Mathew Brady Collection, National Archives and Records Administration, Washington, DC).

Chapter 4, pages 29–36
A Confederate campsite (Photo by Mathew B. Brady in Benson J. Lossing, *History of the Civil War, 1861–65* [New York: War Memorial Association, 1912; repr., Avenel, NJ: Portland House, 1994, 2000], 175).

Chapter 5, pages 37–43
This gunboat, used at the battle of Fort Donelson, was the first ironclad gunboat built in America. It was "armed, supplied, officered and manned" jointly by the Union army and navy.

(Photo by Mathew B. Brady in Benson J. Lossing, *History of the Civil War, 1861–65* [New York: War Memorial Association, 1912; repr., Avenel, NJ: Portland House, 1994, 2000], 257).

Horses killed during a battle in the Civil War (*Frank Leslie's Illustrated History of the Civil War* [New York: Mrs. Frank Leslie, 1895], 462).

Chapter 6, pages 45–51
"Capture of Fort Donelson—Charge of the Eighth Missouri Regiment and the Eleventh Indiana Zouaves, February 15th, 1862" (*Frank Leslie's Illustrated History of the Civil War* [New York: Mrs. Frank Leslie, 1895], 85).

A casualty of the Civil War (Photo by Mathew B. Brady in Benson J. Lossing, *History of the Civil War, 1861–65* [New York: War Memorial Association, 1912; repr., Avenel, NJ: Portland House, 1994, 2000], 239).

Chapter 7, pages 53–63
A "group of Confederate prisoners captured at Fort Donelson on the morning after the surrender" (*Frank Leslie's Illustrated History of the Civil War* [New York: Mrs. Frank Leslie, 1895], 187).

Army transport *Bridgeport*. This is the type of steamboat that was used to transport Confederate soldiers to prison camps during the Civil War. (Photo by Mathew B. Brady in Benson J. Lossing, *History of the Civil War, 1861–65* [New York:

War Memorial Association, 1912; repr., Avenel, NJ: Portland House, 1994, 2000], 357).

This map shows where Johnny Ables's family lived in Calloway County, Kentucky; where the 4th Mississippi Infantry Regiment fought at Fort Henry on the Tennessee River in Tennessee; where Johnny and the Red Invincibles were engaged in battle at Fort Donelson on the Cumberland River in Tennessee; the steamboat route that Johnny and the Confederate prisoners took down the Cumberland River from Fort Donelson to the Ohio River and down the Ohio River to Cairo, Illinois; the train route north from Cairo to Sandoval, Illinois, and east from Sandoval to Vincennes, Indiana; and the two possible train routes from Vincennes to Indianapolis. (Artist's rendition of Civil War–era map by Patricia Prather, Dean Johnson Design, 2005. Based on two maps: "Lloyd's New Military Map of the Border and Southern States" [New York: H. H. Lloyd and Co., 1861]; repr. in Andrew M. Modelski, *Railroad Maps of North America: The First Hundred Years* [Washington, DC: Library of Congress, 1984], 59; and "Section of G. Woolworth Colton's New Guide Map of the United States and Canada with Railroads, Counties, etc., Used by General Grant in Marking the Proposed Lines of Operations of the Armies of the United States, 1864" [New York: Julius Bien and Co., 1863]; repr. in *Atlas to Accompany the Official Records of the Union and Confederate Armies, 1861–1865* [Washington, DC: United States Government Printing Office, 1895]).

Chapter 8, pages 65–76

Sumner Cunningham of the 41st Tennessee Infantry encouraged the first prisoners at Camp Morton to march into the prison with dignity. (*Confederate Veteran* 22 [1914]: 9).

"A group of ragtag Confederate prisoners" (*Frank Leslie's Illustrated History of the Civil War* [New York: Mrs. Frank Leslie, 1895], 462).

Chapter 9, pages 77–88

A photograph of Colonel Richard Owen, first commandant of Camp Morton Prison, taken many years after the end of the Civil War (Photo collection, Indiana State Library).

Guards at Camp Morton Prison in Indianapolis, Indiana, during the Civil War (Eugene F. Drake Camp Morton Photographs, ca. 1864–65, P 0388, Indiana Historical Society).

Chapter 10, pages 89–100

Petition written to Colonel Richard Owen requesting that Johnny Ables be freed from prison and allowed to return home (Civil War Miscellany, Indiana State Archives).

Last of the signatures on the petition for John W. Ables (Civil War Miscellany, Indiana State Archives).

Chapter 11, pages 101–111

"Confederate prisoners at Camp Morton Prison nicknamed

this stream, running through the middle of the camp, "The Potomac." (Eugene F. Drake Camp Morton Photographs, ca. 1864–65, P 0388, Indiana Historical Society).

This photograph of Confederate prisoners outside the wooden barracks at Camp Morton Prison, which was taken in the late summer of 1864, shows that prisoners were allowed to hang their wet laundry outside their barracks as Colonel Owen had planned. (Eugene F. Drake Camp Morton Photographs, ca. 1864–65, P 0388, Indiana Historical Society).

Chapter 12, pages 113–123
Letter from Colonel Richard Owen to Governor Oliver Morton explaining Johnny Ables's situation, dated March 18, 1862, with an added testament as to the accuracy of Owen's account. Note the signatures of two of the soldiers from Company C, 4th Mississippi Regiment, who are familiar characters in this story: W. R. (William) Cade and J. E. (Johnny) Roche. (Civil War Miscellany, Indiana State Archives).

This photograph shows a railroad scene very much like the one Johnny must have encountered as he left the custody of Camp Morton Prison and began his journey home. (Depot, Aurora, Indiana, P 0391, Indiana Historical Society).

Afterword, pages 125–134
Sumner Archibald Cunningham in later life (*Confederate Veteran* 22 [1914]: 180).

This monument at Crown Hill Cemetery in Indianapolis, Indiana, marks the graves of the Confederate prisoners who died at Camp Morton. (Photo by Daniel M. Immel).

In 1916 teachers and students of Indianapolis School #45 placed a boulder at the corner of Alabama and Nineteenth streets to mark the site of Camp Morton. The Indiana Historical Bureau installed a marker at the same location in 1962. Both historical markers were later moved to Herron–Morton Place Historical Park near the former site of Camp Morton in Indianapolis. (Photographs by David Turk, Indiana Historical Society).

The Sons of Union Veterans, Benjamin Harrison Camp 356, placed four markers to show where the four corners of the Camp Morton property had been. One of the markers is shown here. (Photograph by David Turk, Indiana Historical Society).

This memorial statue of Richard Owen sits in the Indiana State Capitol in Indianapolis, Indiana. (Photograph by David Turk, Indiana Historical Society).

Selected Bibliography

United States Census Records

1850, 1860, and 1870 Fayette County, Tennessee, Census.

1860 Henry County, Tennessee, Census.

1860 Marshall County, Mississippi, Census.

Documents in the Indiana State Archives

Rosters of companies C and E, 4th Mississippi Infantry Regiment, List of Confederate Prisoners of War in Indiana Camps, 1862, 107–68.

Petition of the 4th Mississippi Infantry to Colonel Richard Owen, March 6, 1862, Confederate Prisoners of War Correspondence, Folder 72.

Letter from Colonel Richard Owen to Governor Oliver P. Morton, March 18, 1862, Confederate Prisoners of War Correspondence, Folder 72.

Letter from Adjutant General Lazarus Noble to Colonel Richard Owen, March 19, 1862, Letter and Order Book No. 1.

Unpublished Diaries

John L. Bodenhamer, transcription, Old Records Department, Pulaski, Tennessee.

Timothy McNamara, transcription, Z515f, Mississippi State Archives, Jackson, Mississippi.

William Wirt Courteney, Manuscript Department, Tennessee State Library and Archives, Nashville, Tennessee.

Books

Albjerg, Victor Lincoln. *Richard Owen, Scotland 1810–Indiana 1890.* Lafayette: Purdue University, 1946.

Cooling, B. Franklin. *Forts Henry and Donelson: The Key to the Confederate Heartland.* Knoxville: University of Tennessee Press, 1987.

Cunningham, Sumner A. *Reminiscences of the 41st Tennessee.* Edited by John A. Simpson. Shippensburg, PA: White Mane Books, 2001.

Dyer, Gustavus W. *Tennessee Civil War Veterans' Questionnaire.* Easley, SC: Southern Historical Society Press, 1985.

Hinson, Hattie Lou, and Joseph R. H. Moore. *Camp Morton 1861–1865: Indianapolis Prison Camp.* Indianapolis: Indiana Historical Society Publications, 3, no. 3. Reprint, Indiana Historical Society Press, 1995.

Howell, H. Grady, Jr. *For Dixie Land I'll Take My Stand: A Muster Listing of All Known Mississippi Soldiers, Sailors, and Marines.* Madison: Chickasaw Bayou Press, 1998.

Ingmire, Frances Terry, and Carolyn Reeves Ericson. *Confederate POWs: Soldiers and Sailors Who Died in Federal Prisons and Military Hospitals in the North.* St. Louis: Ingmire Publications, 1984.

Jennings, Dorothy, and Kerby Jennings. *The Story of Calloway County, 1822–1976.* Murray, KY: Self-published, 1980.

Long, E. B., and Barbara Long. *The Civil War Day by Day: An Almanac 1861–1865.* Garden City, NY: Doubleday, 1971.

National Park Foundation. *The Complete Guide to America's National Parks, 1990–91.* New York: Prentice Hall, 1990.

Rowland, Dunbar. *Military History of Mississippi, 1803–1898: Taken from the Official and Statistical Register of the State of Mississippi, 1908.* Reprinted with index by H. Grady Howell Jr., Spartanburg, MS: The Reprint Co., 1978.

Secretary of War. *The War of the Rebellion: A Compilation of the Official Records of the Union and Confederate Armies.* Washington, DC: Government Printing Office, 1880.

Thompson, Ed Porter. *History of the Orphan Brigade.* Louisville: L. N. Thompson, 1898.

Periodicals
Confederate Veteran, February 1897, June 1913, July 1913.
Daily State Sentinel, February 27, 1862; March 4, 1862.
Indianapolis Daily Journal, February 24, 1862; March 8, 1862.
Lafayette Daily Journal, February 27, 1862.
The Southern Bivouac, October 1882.

Suggested Reading
Wiley, Bell I. *The Life of Johnny Reb, the Common Soldier of the Confederacy. The Life of Billy Yank, the Common Soldier of the Union.* New York: Book-of-the-Month Club, 1994.